DARK TALES
OF TIME AND SPACE

DARK TALES
OF TIME AND SPACE

SEAN WRIGHT

A Crowswing Book

To my ancestors, who have blazed a trail…

First published in 2005 by Crowswing Books.

PO BOX 301 King's Lynn Norfolk PE 33 0XW England

10 9 8 7 6 5 4 3 2 1

www.crowswingbooks.co.uk

First Edition

ISBN 1-905100-01-9 hardback

(Limited to 470 copies worldwide)

ISBN 1-905100-10-8 hardback slipcased

(Limited to 30 copies worldwide)

ISBN 1-905100-12-4 paperback

(Limited to 1000 copies worldwide)

Printed and bound in Great Britain by Biddles, King's Lynn, Norfolk

Also by Sean Wright

Praise for Sean Wright

'*Jaarfindor* is a compact dark fantasy that's as imaginative as his *Jesse Jameson* series, and reminiscent in style of a cross between something by Michael Moorcock and by Mervyn Peake.' *Hilary Williamson, bookloons.com*

'Just finished *Jaarfindor* and I have to say I was truly captivated. Without being too gushing you really are a wonderful storyteller-I lived that book! I do read quite a lot, especially older fantasy. The imagination and flow was tremendous.' *Gary Power, author*

'What a cracking read...*Jaarfindor*! Multi-layered, fast paced and without a dull moment in sight... Reminiscent of Philip K. Dick's, 'Do Androids Dream of Electric Sheep' - 'Blade Runner.' More addictive than the entire contents of Lia-Va's bag of Roots, I simply couldn't put this book down.' *Lee, Cafe 22, Brighton*

'Sean Wright's *The Twisted Root of Jaarfindor* is one to watch out for...along with Michelle Paver's *Wolf Brother*, PB Kerr's *Children of the Lamp*, Madonna's *The Adventures of Abdi*, Julia Donaldson's *Gruffalo's Child*, Charmian Hussey's *Valley of Secrets*, and Philip Pullman's *Scarecrow and the Servant,' The Observer*

'Highly collectable.' *Book and Magazine Collectors (July Edition 2004)*

'Outstanding fiction of the highest calibre.' *Lucy Masters, Hatchard's Piccadilly*

'Dark, thought provoking, addictive, and with characters and a plot you won't forget in a hurry. Guaranteed to cause a stir.' *Nigel Eastman, sqwubbsybooks.co.uk*

Contents

Introduction

I once said that introductions were pointless waffle or words to that effect. I still believe that. Nothing has changed – much. But some of the time, they illuminate a text, just like a good torch with a brand new Duracell battery might illuminate a dark attic. That illumination comes here in the form of historical context. To me, this book is definitely a dark attic – disturbing secrets, forgotten oddities, and the ever-present menace of being watched, eyed, stalked as possible prey. It's also easier to set any kind of record straight if you do it yourself, I find. So here goes...

This book was written during the autumn and winter months 2004/2005. I owe a debt of gratitude to many people who assisted me in one way or another in tightening up the text of *Dark Tales*, including Trisha Wright, John Wright, Keith and Linda Cole, Helen Lenney, Gail Calvert, Karen Lefever, and the wonderful editorial skills of Elastic Press publisher, Andrew Hook. Thanks also to the University of Chicago Illinois and their links to a variety of hip-hop archive sources, which included slang dictionaries, teaching resource links (such as *The Evolution of Rap Music in the United States* by Henry A. Rhodes at the Yale-New Haven Teachers Institute), and general background information. The NDE research was conducted from a variety of sources, both on-line and from good-old-fashioned text books. Particularly helpful were Dr. Raymond Moody's books and research, spanning many decades. He is acknowledged widely to be the first medical professional to explore near-death experiences. In fact, Dr. Moody coined the phrase Near-Death Experience, or NDE.

I first read Dr. Moody's ground-breaking *Life After Life* in 1978 or 1979. Like many teenagers I was seeking that 'something' beyond the every day drudgery of life. Like many people of that time, I saw Uri Geller bending spoons on TV and didn't really care whether it was a magician's sleight of hand or some aspect of a powerful mind-energy at work. As a spotty teenager, it looked pretty cool. Just imagine being able to do that at a party, I thought. Impressive.

In *Dark Tales of Time and Space*, (just as in my previous teenage-adult book, *The Twisted Root of Jaarfindor*) I've attempted to fuse a 'couldn't careless' attitude with a 'seeking' pre-occupation that many teenagers still have today. It's that enquiring mind, searching beyond the status quo that I believe has led us to many remarkable technological, scientific and perceptual changes. In short, the questioning rebel is without doubt preferred to the mindless hooligan.

Whereas *Jaarfindor* is set in a self-contained fantasy world entirely of my own imagination, *Dark Tales* is very much set in the here and now of the early 21st Century and has a contemporary feel. The fantastic elements come from sources other than my imagination this time, although I'd like to think that my handling of the research material is somewhat imaginative.

Joey Steffano and his dark double, Crack Boy, are the protagonists I have chosen to characterise against a world of possibilities – the great unknown. Life after death, its possible landscapes, its possible infra-structures, its possible ethos is a cultural and religious minefield. Religion, both organised and less structured, tackles the question of life after death in many ways. The idea of a saviour, a conduit through which salvation may be obtained, is the central notion of Christianity. Another idea is that of karma, the reaping of what one has sown through actions, words and thoughts. Intriguing *ideas* indeed.

The third element which I made considerable use of in this book was the unknown, and the *unknowable* – now those notions engaged me as a writer. I've tried to utilise the scientific research of Dr. Moody in a subtle way and marry it with the ever-present onslaught of celebrity. It's everywhere, isn't it? TV reality shows, internet news home pages, and tabloid press. It's an old realisation but worth saying again in the context of this book: is celebrity the new religion; celebs the new icons to be worshiped? Maybe. Or are people more fickle? This seems to me to be more accurate. While teenagers attach their allegiances to a wide variety of music, celebrity, sports teams, designer brands, how long does this last? I hope somewhere along the line that our obsession with celebrity, especially the desire to know all there is to know about a celeb's personal life, may have some kind of evolutionary purpose.

What that is *exactly* is beyond me. Is it that we are simply curious about one another? Or are there far more sinister connotations? Do we perhaps crave the details of a celeb's life to reflect our own status and standing? Perhaps we have an unquenchable thirst for approval, of what we are and what we do? Could it be we seek to dig out the dark side of a celeb's life to understand our own, or is it an act of acquiring dirty ammunition against them?

Dark Tales of Time and Space was chugging along agreeably when something so shocking happened that it wrenched my mind horribly. That event focused me so intensely on the content of this book, that in many ways it became a working metaphor. The Asian tsunami on Boxing Day 2004 will always be a sad day for so many, but in the aftermath of what unfolded on our TV screens and internet connections it affected me deeply. A deep desire to do something to help the victims and their families became paramount. I became centrally involved in the *Book Aid Tsunami Earthquake Appeal* with Crowswing, and many generous authors, artists, photographers, book dealers and publishers from around the world donated signed books and artwork to auction on the internet. No doubt, many of you helped in whatever way you were able. Thank you.

A special thanks to Lee Walker who contacted both me and Nigel Eastman just days after the Tsunami with the idea of a book auction to raise funds; and thanks to Nigel for rounding up some highly collectable books.

Back to the book.

There is strong language in *Dark Tales*, some violence, horror and lots of speculation about the after life. It is for 15+ age range. This book – like my previous teenage-adult crossover *Jaarfindor* – is not for the delicate of heart, or for those who find it difficult to have their preconceived ideas challenged. I find that a questioning mind is a healthy preoccupation.

I'd love to think that *Dark Tales of Time and Space* challenges several cultural stereo-types of organised religion, the possibility of life after death and what that might mean for us as individuals and as a society. The blurb on the book cover reads something like this: *the only border is your mind; the only barrier: your imagination.* If I believe anything at all, then I believe those two phrases the most. But these notions are probably one writer's stab in the dark, one writer's stumbling efforts to discover what remains hidden in the attic when the torch battery runs out. I'll let you be the judge – as always. Enjoy.

Sean Wright – February 2005

Chapter One

Silver Dollar

1

Joey Steffano leapt up on stage from the mosh pit like a cheetah bringing down its prey. He whorled on the heel of his Nike trainers, grabbed the mic-stand and hit the rap with perfect timing. He ran his fingers through his cropped peroxide blonde hair and struck a pose. He was a god on stage. He knew it – his fans knew it. They screamed and he screamed back at them. His wide brown eyes sparkled as a blue-white spotlight hit his black face. He waved his free hand in the air and fifteen thousand fans mirrored his action, waved back. He grabbed his crotch and thrust his pelvis forward in time with the thumping rhythm. He was screwing all of them. The legs of his baggy khaki trousers flapped like sails. His camouflaged flak-jacket swung back and forth. He tapped the reversed white baseball cap on his head three times. He hit the 'Live Life, Die Young' motif on his white t-shirt with his middle finger, and then gave the audience the bird. He rapped:

'Distant machine guns pound da' rats under da' ground, like crooks from the estates where I come from, born in England, raised in Little Italy, boss of the Breakers, bossin our street corner, standing shoulder to shoulder with Mikey J against da' thugs, The Snakeheads, but I ain't runnin, I ain't turnin, I ain't

jerking my chain, no way, I'll just spit back at the rain of mortar bomb shells, just like the bitch, Michelle, utilized laser illumination to home in on her target, I'll ask it, but you ain't listening, you never listen, so how you gonna understand my dilemma? You ever seen my Delirium tremens? I ain't clever, stoned out of my brain, crawling through the mud and rain, such a shame, I have to leave you this way, with a bullet through my brain, but I guess my claim to fame will burn, snuffed out like a premature flame, cause sooner or later, you'll get my message, dig in, keep your head down, don't give in, don't you follow leaders, they all traitors, they all dissin cheaters, users, liars and abusers of the power they wield, use it like a shield to fulfil their own agenda, justify their own benders, when they should be empowering the people who put them in the driving seat, unifying black and white, yellow and red, the Middle East and mainland America, break the cycle of pain, snap the link and the chain around our necks, the noose and the net, will be unshackled, let us be free, to live as we please-'

Joey glimpsed the silver missile out of the corner of his eye. But he turned his head much too late. The razor-sharp coin hit his temple, ripping open the flesh and burying itself into his skull. The pain was intense and blinding. He slapped a hand against his head and pulled it away, staring in disbelief at the blood squirting onto his palm.

Later, Joey would come to think about the swirling, ultra-fast events that had led up to the attack. Some freak in the first three rows had been mouthing something abusive, spittle flying in thick white flecks from his muted lips. The music was pounding and Joey was rapping, not really taking in the guy fully. But he was there. It was a kind of subliminal awareness, a sixth sense. Joey was used to crazies. He blanked them, never maintaining eye contact for more than a few seconds. He refused to give them what they wanted. He was too busy flirting with the blonde babe next to the freaks, whose huge breasts were bouncing up and down in time to the beat. The crazies always got to gigs early and positioned themselves where they knew they would be seen. This one had a particularly evil stare, fixed glaring eyes, an insane hatred. He was wearing a khaki baseball cap and he was whiter than snow. His eyes were pink and the tufts of hair sprouting out from under the cap were as white as his own peroxide mop. Joey had seen the nut raise his hand and take aim. He was an albino. Probably a shamutant, he thought, though he wasn't sure why.

He had taken the full force of the missile. He sprawled backwards, the mic-stand lurching. His legs gave way and his dead weight carried him down heavily. The women in the front row were screaming before his head hit the corner of the stage monitor. More blood squirted out of his wound. More women screamed in the front rows as blood splattered them. Joey Steffano jerked and convulsed. He was violently sick. His tongue wriggled like a purple eel hanging from a fisherman's hook. Glaring footlights shone in his eyes.

The band behind him stopped playing. Roadies and security guards ran onto the stage, some leapt into the crowd, fists flailing toward the albino who'd vented his hatred so accurately. He stood out amongst the many black kids in the front rows; he was no shamutant. His psychic powers were nil.

19

But Joey didn't see any of this. He didn't hear the announcement over the PA system that demanded calm. He didn't see or hear the hysteria in the crowd, the screaming and crying and swearing and confusion. He didn't feel his manager, Jack O'Toole, fumbling for his pulse, or the paramedics carrying him away on the stretcher. He wasn't aware of the blaring sirens as he was rushed to St. Mary's Hospital. If it had been possible for him to think of such things, the silver dollar embedded in his skull would have struck him as ironic. For the millions of dollars he had made in his meteoric rise had not saved him from a single lethal silver dollar. The world's richest, youngest hip-hop-rock star was dead. Joey Steffano had become an icon and a legend thirteen days before his twentieth birthday. He had joined John Lennon, James Dean and Kurt Cobain.

2

Yes! You read that right – the supposedly dangerous, ill-mannered, child-corrupting 19 year old Anglo-American Boy that is Joey Steffano is much loved by my own Mother, and…he's dead!

Having recently read Flashcam's opinion on this man I felt compelled to write my own, having also recently seen Joey Steffano play live at the Reading Rock Festival.

Real name Joseph White, Joey Steffano is also known as alter-ego Crack Boy, which some people find pretty confusing! He has shot to fame over the last couple of years or so due to his controversial lyrics as a black hip-hop-rocker grown up in the 'hood, as they say. He plays with guns, he plays with drugs, he swears like fuck knows what, he hates Bush, detests war and organised religion – allegedly. How much of this is true or merely exaggerated may never be known by your average punter but this is certainly not the first, nor will he be the last, to coax such controversy.

So far I only have his "Crack The Line" LP though I intend to soon buy his "One Pill Too Many" album! I have reviewed the album elsewhere so I won't repeat myself about it. So what of this phenomenon? He's only a little guy with short peroxide blonde hair and innocent eyes – my Mother thinks he's cute and probably just misguided! True his lyrics are plagued with expletives but these days you'll find that to some degree with a lot of non-pop bands who are "real" bands, it doesn't really shock that much these days, does it? I mean, you do remember the Sex Pistols from 25 years ago right? I mean, even John Lennon swore – "Working Class Hero" anyone?

I don't think we can deny, if they listen beyond the swearing, that his lyrics are very cleverly put together, with well constructed songs and more than a large pinch of humour in many cases. He often utilises South Park and The Simpsons voices and references – two cartoons which also were seen as controversial initially. Now on to his live show! Even my hard-rockin', heavy metal loving girlfriend agreed that his live show at the Reading festival was great! He appeared on the bill after Eminem (who also evokes similar criticism and controversy) so it was quite a night. On stage he performed with fellow hip-hop-rock band K 40 and came across as actually quite a friendly, humorous and likeable guy. There was an interval in the middle of his show in which he screened a "Crack Boy" cartoon show in South Park-Simpsons style which was amusing (though not for children maybe – although there were many in the audience).

There was a family behind me with a young boy who was obviously a fervent fan and his mother was giving him the appropriate "guidance" throughout the show – he can listen to 'those' words but it was not OK to say them.' He was undeniably very entertaining with a lot of on-stage interaction with K 40 and use of inflatables, fireworks, cannons spraying out glitter/confetti – he knows how to put on a show and it was going down a storm. He even had Eminem on stage singing "Kick Arse Like a Soldier" with him at one point and how strange they looked together.

The only criticism I could level myself is that I found the hip-hop-rock music a little grating after a while as I prefer guitar-based rock music. I found it a little monotonous in places but at those moments it was best to concentrate on the lyrics and the whole show to overcome that.

In my opinion, I reckon any controversy would have died down in time whether it was deserved or not if Joey Steffano had lived. But Joey Steffano will never become a well-established star now in his field and my Mother will continue to wear her Joey Steffano t-shirt with pride! The albino fuck that killed him with a single silver dollar has created an icon, and that makes me sick because so many people still love Elvis like he was God or something. Will Joey Steffano still be loved in twenty years time by millions of fans?

3

Joey peered over the shoulder of the guy who was reading *Rolling Stone* magazine. Joey was sitting behind him on a slow-moving train. He had no memory of boarding the train, but strangely he didn't feel panicked.

He wasn't sure why. It didn't make sense. Like a series of unrelated dreams in the moments before waking, it felt…well, almost normal. Almost.

Habit kicked in. He felt for his Nokia mobile phone and flick knife. Good. One in the left, and the other in the right front pocket of his trousers. He also felt the keys to his silver Porsche Carrera GT 2005 in his right pocket, too.

'Seen enough?'

Joey eased back into his seat. He felt like a voyeur caught in the act of something terribly sordid. He stared out the window. Where was he? It was a flat and featureless landscape, with stands of aspens and shimmering dykes and freshly ploughed dark earth. Low on the distant blue horizon he saw a bright light, no more than a shining, brilliant speck. He thought it must be the sun's light reflected on a mirror.

'Impressed?' the passenger in front of him said. He turned and poked his bald head between the headrests. 'What's wrong, rock star? You dumb?'

'Where am I?' Joey said, thinking, straining so hard to recall where he'd been before this train journey. It was just out of reach. Nope. Can't think. He rubbed his forehead, which was pounding furiously.

'You're on a slow train, hip-hop man,' the *Rolling Stone* reader said, laughing. 'Did you like your obituary?'

'What?'

'For a multi-millionaire hotshot, you are stupid, aren't you, son?' The *Rolling Stone* reader narrowed his dark brown eyes. His brow furrowed – blacker than Joey's skin, older, too. Much older. But there was no grey hair – just shiny baldness. And a shiny gold sovereign ring on the little finger of his left hand. He was wearing a knee-length black leather coat that Bono from U2 would have been proud of. For an old guy, he looked cool.

'That wasn't an obituary,' Joey said.

The passenger shrugged. 'Reviews and obituaries are all the same thing to me, man. Simple fact is this: you're dead, Joseph White. That's your real name – right? Weird or what?'

Joey looked at him nonplussed. What was this all about? How did he know so much about him? And then he caught himself, scolded himself because millions of people knew a hell of a lot about Joey Steffano from the press and the TV. Perhaps the guy was a celeb stalker?

'Who are you?' he said as casually as he could. He didn't want the jerk to think he'd got him rattled.

The *Rolling Stone* reader ignored the question. 'Or should I call you, Joey Steffano? Maybe you'd like Crack Boy? Which name you claiming today, son? Which alter-ego you living through right now?'

Joey rubbed his hands together. They felt solid. Real. He bit his bottom lip and felt pain. I'm not dead, he thought. This guy is full of bullshit. 'I'm alive,' Joey said.

'You're dead son. Sooner or later you're gonna come to accept that fact.'

The word reverberated through Joey's mind like a rock hitting the hard ground at the bottom of a cartoon canyon.

Dead! *Sooner or later you are gonna come to accept that fact.* DEAD!

'That's right, son. You just like me – we're D.E.A.D. This is the slow train to Journey's End.'

For a split second – no more than that – the *Rolling*

Stone reader phased in and out of Joey's vision. It was as if he'd become transparent momentarily, and then solid again. In that split second, Joey had seen right through him. But it wasn't the seat he'd seen, or any part of the train. It was darkness – a vast dark hole that seemed to impossibly encapsulate everywhere; everything all at once. Absurd.

'I'm dreaming,' Joey said, panic swelling in his heart. The gulf of darkness, a mere glimmer of an image really, had set off a sudden irrational fear inside. It puffed up like something primeval, something fundamental and survivalist. His throat tightened.

'This is a dream.'

'If you say so, son.'

The *Rolling Stone* reader turned back to his magazine. He flicked through the pages.

Joey scrambled to his feet and lurched. He broke out in a sweat, flushed hot and red. He felt a panic-attack coming. His heart was palpitating, his brow beaded with sweat. It was the deep dark nothingness which had started it. He knew this, but his fear had taken on a life of its own.

He staggered along the aisle. He hated confined spaces, hated to be closed in, hated to be out of control. He had fought all his life to control everyone and everything in his world. He'd fought hard and had never taken his eye off his goal, not for one second. He'd won, when others had given up, or lost, or quit. He'd believed in his talent, however raw. He was Joey Steffano, Crack Boy, Joseph White! He was a teenage hip-hop-rock legend, icon, video star, idolised by millions and hated by millions more –

mainly middle-aged white men who'd never taken risks. He was rich beyond belief, sickeningly successful for a kid from a working-class broken home. He was Joey Steffano. He'd made three multi-platinum albums and had been number one in the album and singles charts in every country in the Western world. He was going to be bigger than Elvis by the time he was twenty-one. He had to be bigger than Elvis. Only then would his dope-taking bitch of a mother show him the respect which he deserved.

Look at me, mamma, I'm a freakin' superstar! Who's Elvis now, mama? Who's the main man?

That's what he'd said when he picked up his Best-Newcomer MTV Award at sixteen years old. He won it the next year for best album, and the next for best album and single and video. The national music press and the tabloids had loved his outburst. The mother-son, love-hate story line was one they could milk – rags to riches, young man triumphs over a tragic childhood. The mother-son stories made headlines across the world. Sales of his albums spiralled upward and merchandise deals were struck on the back of his 'hood mentality. His world tours were huge box-office successes. Joey Steffano was a teenage idol.

He wiped sweat from his brow with the back of his hand and swallowed hard. His head was spinning; the walls seemed to close in. He hated small spaces, hated trains, with all their tight confinement. Even the toilets were so small that you needed to be a fucking midget to feel comfortable. Comfortable? Who was he kidding? Those fuckers reeked all the time, even after the cleaner had been in there with a mop and bucket. Why couldn't people hit the bowl? Trains were disgusting places. Filthy germ-riddled sardine cans. Stinking. He hated trains. He had to get off. He had to throw up.

He reached the toilet, pushed the button and the door swished open. He barely managed to stumble inside before he heaved. Nothing came up. He heaved again. No, nothing.

He swallowed hard and turned on the tap. Perhaps if he drank some water, then he'd have something to throw up.

He shook his head. Typical. The tap wasn't working. No water.

He backed out of the toilet and pressed the button to close the door. It whooshed shut.

The train was gathering speed.

Click-clack.

Clickety-clack. Clickety-clack.

He looked up the aisle. All the seats ahead of him were empty. He looked back along the aisle and drew in a sharp, shocked breath. He staggered back a few paces, shaking his head in disbelief.

4

Where there should have been more carriages or a door at the very least, there was nothing. Joey reeled at the sight. He actually winced as if a needle had been jabbed hard into his gum. He sucked in air through his teeth. Less then ten feet away, the train had been ripped in half. Splintered, jagged metal fringed a hole of blackness. It looked like deep space, but there were no stars visible –

just the darkness.

Joey backed off, worried. What the hell was going on here?

He sidled up to the window where he'd been sitting and looked out behind him. This was weird. The flat featureless landscape he'd seen earlier stretched back as far as his eye could see. It reminded him of the fens near Wisbech or the run out near the power plant from King's Lynn station in Norfolk. He'd taken that line to King's Cross many times as a twelve-year-old to visit his father, Ken White. A year later his mother met an American air-force navigator – Eddie Steffano. They got married in a hurry, left for New York's Little Italy, had twins, and argued and fought continuously with each other. Joey spent his teenage years locked in his bedroom, listening to hip-hop and rock or chilling on the street after dark with the crew called the Breakers. He got kicked a lot in the first six months – strange British accent did that mainly. The guys hated it, but the chicks? Joey was a big hit with the girls. But he adapted, changed his accent, his attitudes and took control of The Breakers a month before his fourteenth birthday. It was his rhyming and rapping that had swayed it with Mikey J, the biggest, meanest kid in the gang. No one messed with Mikey J. But he never wanted to be the boss. He wasn't smart enough for that. His only talent was smashing heads and breaking jaws. He stood tall when everyone else around him shrank. His strength allowed Joey to lead. The Breakers displayed their identity and unity in obvious ways. They wore gold sovereign rings, heavy gold neck chains, black jeans, black t-shirts and black leather jackets. Joey thought they looked cooler than ice. They had their own personal jargon and signals common to most gangs.

Joey remained together with the ten to fourteen members (gang membership fluctuated now and again) in quiet times as well as in conflict. The Breakers' main source of income was narcotics. But Joey could see that that road was a one way journey to nowhere. Living in constant fear of conflict was stressful. He'd lost three gang members in drive-by shootings. There had to be another way out of the street.

Joey spent more time rehearsing as he approached his fifteenth birthday. He got off on West Coast gangsta-rapper, Snoop Dogg and Detroit's Eminem, and he thought stadium rock band U2 had something worthwhile to say. He cut a three song demo disc and performed a showcase gig for Jack O'Toole, a highly connected manager whose mouthful of gold-capped teeth earned him the nickname of Sharkey. Joey's own brand of music broke him free from the street with a recording deal with multi-national BVK. Sharkey negotiated a three album deal with a seven figure advance. That kind of up-front investment meant that newcomer Joey would have the full backing of every arm of the BVK hit-making machine. They wanted a good return on their investment. Joey, of course, took the Breakers with him, made them part of his entourage.

Click-clack.

Clickety-clack. Clickety-clack.

The train was moving faster, rhythmically.

He turned, steadied himself by grabbing the velvety maroon headrests, and staggered across the carriage to the other side. He was alone now, and that felt odd. He and his gang were brothers, they were crew. Perhaps he'd had his drink spiked and had been kidnapped by The Snakeheads. He wouldn't put it past them. They were always stepping on each other's turf.

The train was really zipping along now. He peered out the window. More flat landscape greeted him, vanishing beyond to a distant horizon of blue. He was struck by the absence of people from the scenes which flitted past his eyes.

Click-clack.

Clickety-clack. Clickety-clack.

He turned to the *Rolling Stone* reader, with a hundred questions on his lips, but the arsehole had vanished. Joey scanned the carriage up ahead of him – empty. He didn't want to look back to where he knew the head-trip vision would be. But he had to make sure.

He didn't see the distant shimmering light, moving faster and growing larger on the darkening horizon.

Chapter Two

Dark Double

1

Slowly he twisted his neck and saw it out the corner of his eye. Shit! It was still there, a deep vast black hole that opened in to what? Space? An abyss? He didn't know; he didn't want to know. He wanted more than anything right now to get off the train.

He fumbled in his pocket for his Nokia. He prised it out and pressed the speed dial. Nothing. Absolutely nothing at all. Blank. No message saying *SIM card not ready*, nothing.

That happens sometimes Joey said to himself. He'd been in supermarkets and on trains going through tunnels when his phone had cut out. He never got a signal on the tube. There were 'blank' spots where the signal was low or non-existent. Perhaps the black hole had nullified his phone. Whatever, he wasn't too worried about it. Once his phone was working again he'd call up Mikey J. He'd get it sorted out soon enough.

Click-clack.

Clickety-clack. Clickety-clack.

Lurching along the aisle he moved quickly away from the hole. Maybe there would be other passengers in the carriages ahead of him. He shoved a niggling thought away: what if there were no other carriages ahead of him?

2

He reached the end of the carriage a few moments later. He cupped his hands to his face and peered through the double glass doors to the next compartment. It looked as if it was empty.

He pushed the silver button and the doors flew open with a deep hissing sound. He stepped gingerly into the space between the two carriages. His heart thumped with trepidation. What if the door behind him whooshed shut, locking him between the two compartments?

In front of him, the door hissed open.

Joey stepped inside the carriage, scanning left and right along the tops of the headrests. The door hissed shut behind him.

He bobbed down low enough to look beneath the seats. There were no legs dangling. The carriage was empty. He studied the overhead baggage racks as he walked as quietly as possible along the length of the carriage. No baggage. No people. He was alone.

But now he was quite a way from the hole. He took out his Nokia again and pressed the speed dial. Perhaps... Still no signal. Just a blank grey screen. He put the Nokia away and strode on.

When he reached the next carriage he paused and peered in, hands cupped as before, squinting through the glass door. This carriage wasn't completely empty. He could see heads about a third of the way down the compartment. There were people in there.

He pushed the button on the wall and the doors swished open. He stepped inside the carriage and strode steadily toward the people. There were half dozen or so dotted around, talking. They didn't seem to notice him. Nothing unusual about that, he thought. Trains were intimidating places, where minding your own business was for the best.

Click-clack.

Clickety-clack. Clickety-clack.

The train was gathering even more speed.

Joey sat down opposite the first couple he came across. They were deep in conversation and didn't acknowledge him either. The woman was strikingly beautiful, hypnotic, memorable.

Everything here in this carriage seemed normal. Perhaps The Snakehead's had spiked his drink with Rohypnol, packed him on this train without his knowledge, and he was now hurtling across mid-America. He wouldn't put it past them. They had a sick sense of humour.

He dragged his eyes from the beautiful woman opposite and gazed out of the window. The landscape was changing. Light – amber to yellow-silver – glistened from the thin dykes. Streamers of blue-grey mist tumbled from an invisible mouth. Factories from a bygone age whizzed by – Victorian blurs before his eyes. He thought that this was strange, because the landscape's features looked neither like England nor America. His mid-American Snakehead kidnapping scenario was blown away. A distant windmill's sails were frozen. Mist rose and undulated, worming its way between trunks in woodland. Blurred oaks and rows of aspen reached up from the earth. Dirty black strips of ploughed land were cut and dissected by dykes brimming with water.

He took out his Nokia again. He had to call Mikey J. He'd make sense of this crazy train ride. Perhaps I've been drugged with Ketamine by The Snakeheads and I'm hallucinating.

He slammed the Nokia into his open palm. It was still not working.

The train was picking up more speed now and the landscape flashed by.

Clickety-clack. Clickety-clack.

The couple opposite were discussing articles in detail from the *Washington Post*, adding knowledge from their memories about a child being taught in a three square yard cubicle. She had an allergy to cosmetic smells. Shampoo and soap and perfume aromas caused asphyxiation.

The woman read aloud, much to Joey's annoyance. At least she was American, which added more mystery to Joey's English landscape theory. He pretended to gaze out the window, but watched her attractive reflection. She was perhaps thirty, with a sleek jaw-line, blue eyes, and wavy red hair. She wore a sheepskin coat, and brown leather gloves.

'The White House called the attack another "desperate" act by terrorists and Saddam Hussein loyalists seeking to derail national elections, slated for Jan. 30th, and the establishment of democracy in Iraq,' she said.

The older guy next to her, flecks of white in his brown hair, nodded and hmmmed.

'Listen to what the sad arse Bush has the audacity to say,' she said evenly. She mimicked a Texan accent.

'"Any time of the year it's a time of sorrow and sadness when we lose life. This time of year is particularly sorrowful for the families as we head into the Christmas season. We pray for them," Bush said.

'"We send our heartfelt condolences to the loved ones who suffer today. Just want them to know that the mission is a vital mission for peace. The idea of a democracy taking hold in what was a place of tyranny and hatred and destruction is such a hopeful moment in the history of the world."'

'You crack me up, Ellen,' he said, and moved his hand to her thigh, squeezing. He spoke in a clipped English accent. 'You're so funny.'

'Why thank y'all, Harry.'

Harry threw his head back like a horse and laughed so loud that many of the passengers twisted around to see where the noise was coming from.

He patted Ellen's thigh and winked.

'You can do that Yankee accent tonight, darling,' he said in a tone that made Joey want to throw up.

'Yankee's a northern American thing, darling,' she said almost in a whisper. 'Bush baby is from Texas – a southerner.'

'You know so much, Ellen,' he said admiringly. His hand moved higher up her thigh. 'And you're so good at it.'

Joey coughed away a snigger, rubbing his palm across his face to hide his embarrassment. Sick old perv, he thought. But from Ellen's flushed face and sparkling, lively eyes, she didn't seem to mind. In fact, she was revelling in his mock adolescent attention. Harry wasn't the best-looking guy in the world, Joey thought. Far from it. So what did she see in him? Perhaps she liked the fatherly type?

Her face became serious as she read aloud from the newspaper again.

Joey hoped she wasn't going to read the entire newspaper out loud. Despite her stunning looks, she was grating on him.

'The exact cause of a massive explosion that ripped apart a mess hall tent during the lunch hour was not immediately known. Initial reports indicated it could have been the result of a mortar attack, a rocket-propelled grenade or perhaps a planted explosive device. The radical Islamic group Ansar al-Sunnah issued a statement claiming responsibility.

'Reports from the scene said at least 90 people were injured in the explosion. Earlier in the week 60 people were killed in two explosions elsewhere in the country.

'More than 1,900 U.S. troops have died in Iraq since the 2003 invasion; more than 11,000 others have been injured.'

'That's awful,' Harry said. 'Those Yanks got themselves into the same mess in Vietnam – only we've bloody joined them this time. What does Blair think he's playing at?'

'God only knows,' Ellen said. 'Too much power for a man so young.'

'It's ridiculous,' Harry said. 'God help him when he snuffs it. He's got a lot to answer for.'

Harry looked up then, caught Joey's eye for a split second. Joey got the message. *A lot to answer for.* Nice one, Harry. He was about to speak, about to ask Harry if he had a beef with him, but Ellen carried on.

'The majority of people in the United States consider that casualty rate unacceptable. According to public opinion polling released Tuesday, 70 percent of 1,004 adults questioned Dec. 16-19 for ABC News and the Washington Post said the goals of the war – ousting Saddam and establishing democracy – did not outweigh the cost in U.S. lives; 56 percent said they believed the war was not worth fighting compared to 42 percent who answered in the affirmative. The negative number was the highest disapproval figure since the March 2003 invasion.

'But despite the human cost and the angst it has caused, 58 percent of respondents were against withdrawing from Iraq until U.S. forces restore civil order in the country. Thirty-nine percent were for early withdrawal. The margin of error for the poll was plus or minus 3 percentage points.

'The polling results, bannered in newspaper headlines and leading many television news broadcasts, differed from a Pew Research Centre Survey earlier in the month in which 44 percent of 2,000 respondents still believed going to war in Iraq was right.'

'Bullshit,' Harry said. 'Statistics can be manipulated in any way you want. Who are these people they poll anyway?'

'Quite,' Ellen said. She laughed, harsh and crow-like. 'Now listen to this classic of stating the bloody obvious from the Whitehouse, darling.

'White House spokesman Scott McClellan said, "Polls are snapshots in time."'

'What?' Harry said, almost in disbelief.

'"Polls are snapshots in time."'

The pair locked eyes and howled with laughter.

'My God,' Harry said, appalled. 'The clowns have taken control of the world and turned it into a freak show circus.'

Ellen nodded and carried on.

'Bush has repeatedly warned that attacks by terrorists and Iraqi rebels would increase as elections drew near. He re-emphasized the point in a news conference Monday when he spoke of the stakes involved in seeing Iraq to democracy.

'"We have a vital interest in the success of a free Iraq," he said. "You see, free societies do not export terror. Free nations are peaceful nations. And free nations in the heart of the Middle East will show what is possible to others who want to live in a free society."'

'What bullshit,' Harry said. 'Free nations are peaceful? Who's he trying to kid? Bush's attack on Iraq was an act of war. A free nation's act of terror. More smoke and mirrors from the magician-clown they call the President.'

Ellen patted Harry's arm. 'Calm down, darling. Remember your blood pressure.'

Let The President answer a higher anarchy, Joey thought, reciting Eminem's words from *Mosh*, his attack on Bush. *Strap him with an Ak-47, let him go, fight his own war, let him impress daddy that way. No more blood for oil, we got our own battles to fight on our own soil, no more psychological warfare, to trick us to thinking that we ain't loyal. If we don't serve our own country, we're patronizing a hero. Look in his eyes. It's all lies. The stars and stripes, they've been swiped, washed out and wiped and replaced with his own face...*

'Listen to this,' Ellen said.

'Bush also said that January voting was not the end of the tunnel. Following the balloting for an interim national assembly, Iraqi legislators would still need to draw up a constitution that would need to be approved by the Iraqi people. Another round of voting would then occur to establish a constitutional government.

'"My point is the elections in January are just the beginning of a process, and it's important for Americans to understand that," he said.

'"The terrorists will attempt to delay the elections, to intimidate people in their country, to disrupt the democratic process in any way they can.

'"No one can predict every turn in the months ahead, and I certainly don't expect the process to be trouble free, yet I am confident of the result. I am confident the terrorists will fail," Bush said.'

Harry shook his head.

'You heard enough, darling?' Ellen said.

I have, thought Joey. He gazed around the carriage. People were dozing, or slipping into sleep with half-closed eyelids, rocking to the motion. A couple of people sitting on different seats, one a young guy dressed in a fading denim jacket, the other a busty brunette in a roll neck sweater, were chatting on mobile phones.

Joey quickly got his Nokia out and hit the speed dial for Mikey J. Nothing.

'You might need a network upgrade,' Harry said to him.

'How come?' Joey said.

'I see you're having problems there with your phone.'

Joey nodded. 'It's blank. Nothing at all.'

'Push 987. You can get an upgrade that way.'

Joey nodded his thanks and thumbed in the digits. He thought that he had all the network coverage money could buy, but perhaps the guy was right. It was worth a try.

The Nokia was still totally dead.

Ellen continued reading her newspaper aloud.

Joey sighed heavily. He was squeezing the Nokia hard. His knuckles were rising from his flesh like small white peaks. He really had heard enough of her voice, and he was sick to his gut of his damn Nokia.

'The question is, how long will people in the United States tolerate the death of its men and women in a conflict so controversial. The polling indicates growing unease, but still a commitment to follow Bush's exhortation to stay the course, not withdraw, perhaps prematurely as Washington did during its Somalia adventure after the death of more than a dozen soldiers in a Mogadishu battle.

'For now, reporters' attempts at the White House to draw a parallel between Tuesday's explosion in Mosul and the 1983 terrorist bombing of the Marine Corps barracks in Beirut that killed hundreds has failed to gel. For now.

'As the White House digested the news of Mosul Tuesday, Bush made the short trip from the White House to the Walter Reed Army Medical Centre to visit wounded service people. It was his seventh visit to the facility. In keeping with previous visits, journalists accompanying The President were kept away as he met with his troops and their families.

'The specific venue at Walter Reed was a Fisher House, a temporary living facility for families travelling long distances to be with wounded loved ones. A Fisher House was opened at Walter Reed in May, with the help of the Fisher House Foundation and the Avon Foundation. More than 600,000 Avon sales representatives sold yellow pins to help raise some of the funds for the building, which was the third one built at the hospital.

'"In Iraq and elsewhere, we've asked a great deal of the men and women of our armed forces," Bush said Monday. "Especially during this holiday season, those on duty far from home will be in our thoughts and our prayers."

'After visiting Walter Reed, Bush added: "And I want to thank the soldiers who are there (in Iraq), and thank those who have sacrificed, and the families who are worried about them during this Christmas season, for their sacrifice. This is a very important and vital mission. I'm confident democracy will prevail in Iraq. I know a free Iraq will lead to a more peaceful world. So we ask for God's blessings on all who are involved in that vital mission."

'Bush later left for Camp David in Maryland, where he was spending Christmas. He would later travel to his ranch in Texas for the New Year holiday.

'The Bush administration has ordered more troops to Iraq. The number is expected to swell to 150,000 to help establish security for the elections.'

Joey looked up at Harry. He was asleep, head thrown back, mouth open.

Ellen patted his hand and read silently now. She

slipped her gloves from her fingers and placed them carefully on the small semi-circular table protruding from the side of the train.

Click-clack.

Clickety-clack. Clickety-clack.

Click-clack…click-clack.

The train was slowing slightly.

Joey saw a bonfire contained in a blackened metal cage, and there were goods-yards of grime and filth. He refocused his eyes into the far distance. There it was again – that small radiant light – moving at a tremendous speed above the tree line.

Closer he saw burnt out cars strewn across lush green fields. Leaves turned gold and burnished were ready to fall. A small block of russet pipes sat indolent in a paddock.

The carriage filled with low whispers, excited, rising. What was happening? The train was slowing down even more. Up ahead, around a small bend, Joey could see a station. Yes, a station! It was his chance to get off.

He got up, clutching his Nokia, and hurried to the exit. Perhaps it would work once he got off of this nightmare ride? The platform was crammed with commuters. The train pulled into the station. Silver metal benches were emptying, busy coffee bars, post office, an information point. All he would need was right here, he thought, feeling sudden relief.

The train stopped.

Now he would take his chance and get off this…what did the freaky old guy call it? That's right, the slow train to Journey's End.

He pushed the button to open the doors. Nothing happened. He pushed the button again, harder this time.

People were getting on the train into the empty carriage next door.

'Shit,' he murmured, and slammed his fist against the door's window. He pressed the button frantically a half dozen times. 'Open!'

More passengers got on, emptying the platform. A station guard stepped out from a door marked 'staff' onto the platform. He was a serious-looking man, dressed in a dirty navy uniform. He raised an orange flag and blew hard on his whistle.

'No,' Joey shouted at him, and pounded the window. 'I want to get off!'

The guard nodded curtly at Joey. That nod said, 'Sure you do, son. But that ain't possible. Now go back to your seat and sit down like a good boy. Just do as you're told, lad. Don't cause trouble.'

Joey turned, slipped his Nokia into his pocket, and sprinted along the aisle toward the carriage where so many people had got onboard. He hit the 'open doors' button.

'Come on, come on. Open up. Open!'

He banged the button again. The doors remained closed. He could see people taking off their coats and putting bags and holdalls into the racks above them.

'Let me in!' he yelled, banging the glass.

A young woman looked up from a book she was reading – Orwell's *Down and Out in Paris and London*. She was slim, in her early twenties, shoulder-length brunette hair, brown eyes, pale unblemished skin. A navy blue beret sat at a jaunty angle on her head. She looked like a résistance fighter.

'Open the door, please,' Joey said. 'I have to get off.'

She got up, placed the open book down onto the seat, and walked to the door. She pressed the button on her side. The doors whooshed open.

'Thanks,' Joey said, almost wanting to kiss her.

He edged by, smelling her heady perfume, and weaved his way through the passengers who were still standing. As he reached the end of the carriage, he came to a grinding halt.

Too late.

The exit doors were already closed. The train lurched out of the station.

He smashed his fists against the glass in the door. He wanted to throw up. The platform guard winked when Joey passed him.

Joey banged his head against the window and roared. He felt the place where the silver dollar protruded from his skull fizz with pain. The glass was cold and his breath made condensation briefly. He closed his eyes and tried to think. He was shaking a little. There had to be a way off the train. Think, man. Think.

The train built up speed quickly and the monotonous rumble of wheels and rails grinding together crammed his mind. He rode the sound, blocked everything but the monotony of wheels and rails. Wheels and rails. Grinding. Sparking. Heating and cooling.

Click-clack.

Clickety-clack. Clickety-clack.

Click-clack.

Clickety-clack. Clickety-clack.

The sound soothed him, helped him to think. He entered another space, a visualisation of calm and logic. It was the place he retreated to when the world around him got too much, overloaded his sensitive artistic brain. It was Joey's place, where songs were born, melodies and lyrics and rhythms came to life in there.

3

'Why don't you try the emergency stop thingy up there?'

Joey remained still, startled by the break in the monotonous clickety-clack of wheels on the track. It was a woman's voice, low but melodic. Her perfume invaded him. It was the woman who'd opened the carriage door for him. It was a distinct aroma – like a baking hot summer's day, fooling around in the freshly cut corn fields of his childhood before the move from England's green and pleasant land to America's harsh city street gang life. Even now Joey could feel his six inch flick knife handle in his front right trouser pocket. Some habits he couldn't shake off.

He lifted his head from the warming glass. He opened his eyes. 'Who are you?' he said.

'Annie,' she said.

'Annie who?'

'Just Annie will do.'

'Sure,' he said, seeing that she didn't want him to pry any further.

He felt for the first time since 'waking,' or whatever it

was, into this reality that he now had someone he could talk to, someone similar to his age, someone who might know what was going on. For the first time Joey was hopeful.

'Do you think the emergency stop will work?' he said.

She looked up at the red handle above them. 'Let's see,' she said.

She reached up, a wicked grin emerging, and yanked it down hard. Her beret was bobbled with wear and tear. Her hair picked up the carriage light, glinted.

'Cool,' Joey said, smiling.

As he'd suspected, the emergency stop didn't work. 'Oh well,' he said, trying to sound composed. 'I'll be ready the next time the train stops. Then I'm out of here.'

Annie brushed her flimsy fringe out of her eyes. She smiled and nodded. They gazed for a few seconds into each other's eyes. Unrelenting. It was enough. For now.

'Do you think the windows open?' Joey said.

'Shall we try them?'

Annie led the way back to her seat and reached up to the window latch. She tugged but it was either very stiff or locked.

'Hey, let me help,' Joey said.

She moved aside and Joey yanked on the latch. It didn't budge. He grabbed it with two hands, but it was locked somehow.

'You think they've locked us in here so they can gas us?' Joey said, not joking.

Annie smiled and shrugged her shoulders. 'I don't think so.' Her fringe flopped over her eyes again. She brushed it away with her fingertips and sat down, moving her book so that Joey could sit next to her.

Joey sat down.

'Who do you think *they* are?' Annie said.

'I'm not sure,' he said, not revealing his Snakehead suspicions. He wanted to pump Annie for all she knew. 'What do you think?'

'I don't know,' she said. 'I never thought of them as they.'

'Them?'

'The people who run this train.'

'Who runs this train?'

'Franklin's in charge and he's helped by a few other volunteers.'

Joey's heart raced at the sound of the name, but he wasn't sure why. He even knew the name. It was embedded in his mind like a Nike advert. 'Franklin J Merryhill?'

'Yes,' she said, her voice rising with excitement. She smiled and turned to Joey, lightly touching his hand and then withdrawing her fingertips. She rearranged her beret. 'You know him, too?'

'I don't think so. I'm not sure how I know his name. I just do. Is he onboard now?'

'He was onboard, but he got off back there.' She looked perplexed for a moment. 'Strange thing about Franklin is how he gets off at a stop, and then appears again a little later, as if he never got off at all. Does that sound odd to…you? I'm sorry. But you didn't tell me your name.'

'Yes, that sounds odd,' he said. 'And my name's Joey – Joey Steffano.'

'Joey,' she said. 'Like the character in *Friends*?'

'No, not like the character in *Friends*. Not at all.'

Joey smiled because she didn't seem to recognise him. That was good. If she didn't know his hip-hop background, that was very good. Neither of them would have an advantage. That's how Joey had come to look at his relationships with people he didn't know. There were those who recognised him instantly, and that was bad. His public image was a sham, of course. He knew it; hell, he had created the facade because that's what sold records. Attitude.

Joey the Stranger appealed to him because the scrutiny of his public and private life by the press had wrung him dry. In the minds of millions, he belonged to them. He hung over beds, glaring down from posters, an extension of a teenage fantasy that most of the kids who got off on him would grow out of eventually. He considered his relationship with his fans as two-dimensional. The commitment was nil the moment he stepped off stage. In many ways, Joey Steffano was a very private guy.

'What does Franklin J Merryhill look like?' he said at last.

'He's black, bald and-'

'Wears a gold sovereign ring on his little finger and has got a cool knee-length leather coat.'

'You do know Franklin,' she said joyfully.

'Yes,' he said. 'I think I do. He likes to read, doesn't he?'

'Yes. He says it helps him learn about people and events that would otherwise pass him by.'

'Right,' Joey said flatly. 'What exactly is it he does on this train?'

Annie smiled with the innocence of a child. 'He rescues people from out there,' she said, pointing. 'That's where they enter the after life – in the Wilderness.'

Joey made a small nervous laugh. 'Right,' he said. 'Did he tell you that *you* were dead, too?'

'That's right. I am dead to my old life. But Franklin rescued me, saved me from the eternal torment of those creatures out there in the Wilderness. There are bad things out there – creatures which can smell the scent of a soul like a wolf smells blood from miles away. I owe Franklin everything. He's my guardian angel.'

'Right,' Joey said, feeling really uncomfortable now. Her hair seemed to lose its sheen.

'We're all dead on this train,' Annie continued. 'Well, actually, if you want to get a little new age about it: we've moved on from one state of being to another, so technically we're still alive. But our old physical bodies are like shells that we've discarded in the never-ending journey of-'

'I get the picture,' Joey said, cutting her sentence up. 'Are you working a scam with that old bald bastard, is that it?'

Annie recoiled at Joey's harsh tone. Her face collapsed with anxiety.

'Scam? What do you mean?'

Joey shrugged and got up, shaking his head. His face was slack with disappointment. 'Are Ellen and Harry in on this, too?'

'What do you mean? In on this?'

Joey backed away from her. He was furious. How could he have let down his guard? He'd been shafted.

What an idiot. She was no résistance fighter; she was compliant and gutless.

Annie got up and reached out to comfort him. Joey knocked her arm away.

'Of course they're in on it,' he said bitterly. He glanced around the carriage. Most of the people onboard were watching him. 'I bet you're all in on it! Who the fuck are you people?'

Still they stared in a pacifist manner. Not zombies exactly, but rather too close for Joey's liking. Their blind acceptance of Franklin's bullshit made him angry. It was as if they'd been hypnotized. Perhaps this was one of those lunatic religious cults that proliferated so many American cities, he thought. Maybe he'd been kidnapped and drugged by The Moonies, or by some animal rights cell who were demanding a huge ransom for multi-millionaire Joey Steffano's safe return?

'Stop staring at me, you arseholes!' he roared.

It wasn't Joey they were staring at, but the dark mirky creature emerging from his naval.

Joey followed their lower gaze and screamed.

'What the fuck is that?'

He tried to knock it aside like a slug or spider that has fallen onto your flesh without you realising. But it wasn't solid. It was a dark cold mist that had grotesque gargoyle features. It corkscrewed up from Joey, hissing and spitting at him. Its eyes were deep red pits, slashed with horizontal pupils of amber.

'Jesus,' he whispered. He was afraid to touch it a second time. 'What is it?'

'The dark half of you,' Annie said. 'Many of us go

through this separation a little while after death. It's your dark double. His name is Crack Boy.'

'Don't talk shit,' he said. But his mind was tumbling now with wild thoughts. Crack Boy? What was this? She was messing with his head. Crack Boy was his alter-ego, like Eminem's Slim Shady. Crack Boy was bad, crazy, addicted to drink and drugs and guns. But Joey Steffano had left all that behind. Crack Boy had been ditched in a Santa Monica Rehab Clinic eleven months ago. He was a bad boy, but he'd been dealt with. He had been tamed. Crack Boy was history.

What was this crap Annie was talking?

'Let the dark double go,' Annie said. 'Let Crack Boy go to the place he belongs.'

Joey turned to her, tears of fear and anger in his eyes. 'I thought I could trust you. But I was wrong. You're as nutty as the rest of them onboard this ghost train!'

'Don't fight it, Joey,' Annie said. 'Let it go. It's full of fear and anger. Crack Boy is searching for the dark.'

Seconds later the creature severed from his naval completely and attacked him savagely. Now Crack Boy felt real and solid. It looked hideous, an ancient and gnarled thing. Like a gargoyle he'd seen as a child, hanging from the grey walls of English churches. Only this grotesque thing was animated and very much alive.

Joey parried its malicious blows away, his arms stinging. But two got through, hitting him in the eye and the side of the head. The physical force wasn't so bad. The punches were no more than hard slaps, but his own emotional response surprised him. He screamed like a child left alone in his bedroom for the first time with the lights turned out.

'Don't fight it,' Annie said. 'Crack Boy wants to break free. Let him go.'

Long ago, Joey had been tricked by a rival gang into accompanying them on a hoax attack on The Snakeheads. He'd been young and gullible, and as he was led down a dead end alley, the seven members of The Razors knocked him to the ground, kicking and punching him. He'd rolled into a ball as tight as he could, head tucked into his lap, hands linked around his head and his arms acting like wings to protect his ribs.

Strangely he felt safe and secure, despite their brutal onslaught. It was probably the foetal position that created the illusion of security, but it was the timely arrival of Mikey J and the rest of the crew that swung the odds in his favour.

He dropped into a tight ball now, praying for Mikey J and the crew to come crashing in through the side window.

It didn't happen.

Instead, he listened to Annie. Despite her crazy talk, her advice was working. He stayed tucked up and as calm as possible. He was acutely aware of his vulnerable body – all of it, it seemed, simultaneously.

The blows stopped.

The creature backed away.

Joey looked up.

Crack Boy was flying at a tremendous speed, seeming to get more solid and denser as it approached the dark hole at the end of the carriage.

A few yards from the hole it landed on the floor of the

train and legs sprouted. It ran and jumped with the grace of a ballerina into the abyss and vanished.

It was a paradoxical image – a dark grotesque creature that moved with poise and artistic grace – that would remain with Joey Steffano for a long time. Crack Boy had gone, but for how long? Joey knew that that part of himself had lurked in the shadows of his mind, always ready to take control when he was weak and tired. Was that really the release of Crack Boy forever?

He shivered.

Or would the dark double return?

Chapter Three

Half-Past Dead

1

As Crack Boy hurried through the dark world, he wasn't aware of Javanah at all. But she pursued him nonetheless.

He had no idea that he'd detached from Joey Steffano, like a new born babe from its mother's umbilical. To his mind, his attack on the 'twin kid,' as he called him, was just one more attack of many attacks on *him*. The 'twin kid' deserved all he got; he had sold them out with his weak-willed appeasements to Jack O'Toole, record company executives, producers, and the press. It could all have been so very different if he'd listened to Crack Boy more often and not those other clowns.

He also had no idea that his features now resembled not a handsome young man but an ancient grotesque creature. One of his hands was a stump, but he couldn't recall if this had always been the case. Perhaps he'd severed his fingers in an accident. Perhaps he was a leper, wasting away. He didn't know.

As always, Crack Boy was busy, busy, busy. He fingered the crevice in his chin with the little finger of his good hand. If he wasn't doing deals with drugs, he was using them; and if he wasn't cutting a new hip-hop groove to make more money to buy more drugs, he was just hanging with his old crew, The Breakers. Despite the fame and fortune, that's what he liked doing best – just hanging with the crew.

But not today.

Today there was something more urgent, more pressing. He had his own selfish needs to sort out. He was coming down, crashing badly, and he hated the feeling. As Mikey J would say when the crew were crashing after coke, he was 'half-past dead.'

He needed another high – fast. He craved drugs and drink – a bottle of vodka would do to start with. He needed to function in the world with a brain buzzing with good thoughts and quality feelings. He wasn't fussy which drugs, but GHB, or Charlie, or rope would be a bonus.

He knew that this place of darkness was all part of the coming down. He knew this landscape well, or thought he did. It was the place he slipped into when the tremors began, when he rocked back and forth in a corner, wrapping his arms around his body, clutching his itchy elbows, feeling like crap, feeling worse than any bout of flu or migraine or toothache. It was also the dark place of visions and hallucinations and nightmares. Just like a dream, or a trip, you never knew when the situation would change. But somehow, this time it felt different – more permanent.

Stop fooling with yourself, he thought. You're just coming down. But still the nagging thought persisted.

He sniffed – unsettled, fidgety – an outward manifestation of his Charlie addiction. But he didn't see it as a problem. It was a means to an end: the ultimate high.

He'd chased that experience ever since his first hit of Charlie, but he had failed to achieve as much pleasure as he did from his first rush. The myth out there said that the first time was the best, and after that, it was all downhill and nose bleeds. He knew the side-effects and the risk to his health. The Santa Monica doctors in the rehab clinic had rattled on about prolonged cocaine snorting resulting in ulceration of the mucous membranes of the nose and that it can damage the nasal septum enough to cause it to collapse. The doctors had showed graphic colour slides of the horrific result of cocaine addiction, and he'd puked with most of the rehab group. But the lure of Charlie was a powerful master, and his mind was expert at locking away the facts in a dark room somewhere in his mind. Just like the two-faced doctors in rehab, who snuck out back to puff on their cigarettes, denying the ill-effects of addiction was easy to do out of the public glare of a rehab group.

'We do the dark things in private,' he muttered, and scanned the vast landscape before him. This was his private world.

The dark world was the deification of all dark worlds, gothic-gloom, foggy, end-less for what seemed like eternity in all directions. It was sinister and colourless, without light except for the dim, misty haze of the outlying city sprawl which etched itself on the horizon. That city was a long way off. But it was full of promised delights. It looked so beautiful – a city of blinding lights.

He saw the track, too. It was not much more than a pathway really. He called it his Yellow Brick Road, an irony Judy Garland would have probably appreciated.

The fact that it was neither yellow nor made of brick didn't matter. This was a strong metaphor for Crack Boy, in a land of oddity, surprises and wonders.

He had followed his personal Yellow Brick Road many times while high on a cocktail of drink and drugs. It was never-ending, or seemingly so. He hadn't passed through poppy fields, although the opium associated with them made him smile. There was no tin-man, or cowardly lion, or brainless scarecrow. Although he'd met many here who could have been described in such two-dimensional terms. He didn't expect to meet a charlatan wizard at the end of it, either.

What he did expect was something far more sinister and addictive. Crack Boy was sure that there were more drugs and drink at the end of it. Some of the coke heads he'd occasionally met in this place spoke in reverent tones about a gigantic warehouse, or a vast nightclub, or a palace where the Ultimate High awaited those lucky enough to make it to Journey's End.

If only he could reach it.

The city's beautiful haze beckoned.

He sniffed and looked along the Yellow Brick Road lined with the swamps which gave nightmares, illusion and pain. There were darker silhouettes, a tangled web of trees, floating creatures. He shivered with a fear of recollection. He'd met dark things in those swamps, had experienced dark deeds off the by-ways and on the bayou. The bayous were teeming with snakes, snapping turtles and alligators.

One moment you could be jogging along the track toward the city sprawl, and then the next everything would change. You never knew when those dream-like sequences would take you.

An occasional crooked sign pointed the way to *Journey's End – the Ultimate High*.

Crack Boy thought that those signs were probably someone's sick joke. No, not someone's – his own sick joke. He was after all acutely aware that this terrain was located *inside* his own head, even though he forgot that sometimes in the intensity of his highs. Was reality separate from his perception, or part of it?

Crack Boy had been hit by slipstream vertigo many times, a kind of melting sensation that made the entire dark world seem permanent, almost a thing that could be hugged. But it slipped time and time again and, like the dark world on which he trudged warily between swamps, he walked on, waiting for the next slippage. He felt depressed, as if nothing was worthwhile. What was the point? He asked himself this countless times. He also felt anxious, as if something bad was about to happen. But it didn't.

He walked hours without any perceivable change in his surroundings, but then everything would change. It was impossible to differentiate between what was 'real' and what was hallucination. Sometimes he felt muscle pains and angry with the smallest things. He also felt extremely tired, but when he tried to sleep, his mind raced with shifting imagery of people's faces and places he'd visited. Like a kaleidoscope. He couldn't rest, no matter how hard he tried.

Sometimes he seemed very close to the city, and then it appeared just as though a distant speck on the horizon. It was almost as if he was a character in a film that had been spliced and edited in a random fashion. There was no linear chronology here in the dark world. Time ceased to be relevant. Space changed and fluxed. A mere whim or a wayward emotion could and did change everything around him. Those unpredictable changes made him feel giddy and nauseous. He puked often on the side of the track.

He passed the miles steadily, not hastening, not mooching about. Each step was one step closer to knowing. He felt irritable and agitated most of the time now. He knew the signs of a downer. He was certainly *half-past dead*, in the parlance of Mikey J. He needed a fix, he craved it more than anything. But his irritability was also in part due to the frustration of the journey on this Yellow Brick Road. Sometimes close, sometimes annoyingly far.

'All is illusion,' he told himself. 'Perhaps I haven't moved at all. Perhaps the moment I leapt from the train into the dark hole I froze solid. Like an ice sculpture. Slowly melting.'

Now where did that one come from? It was a burst of recall that instantly vanished. That seemed to be happening to him more and more of late. He'd remember something from weeks or months ago, and then in an instant – bang!

Lost again.

A camouflaged water canteen was clipped to the army utility belt around his waist. It was almost empty, and he was worried. He was worried because it had been full of Smirnoff vodka.

Luckily at that moment he had no exacting desire to drink. In an indistinct way, this pleased him. But he was no fool. He should have filled the canteen with water, because he knew that very soon the after-effects of the drink and drugs would make him extraordinarily thirsty.

He felt the crevice in his chin, thinking. He looked for a moment at the swamps around him, seemingly everywhere. Ironic that they held so much water, but the coke heads had claimed them to be foul and poisonous. He wondered if they spoke the truth. He doubted it. Maybe need would outweigh all else and he would have to drink from them to quench the mighty thirst that would soon come. Would that drink turn into diarrhoea or worse? He already felt badly dehydrated. If he could reach the city, though, he'd stand a better chance of finding fresh clean water.

Next to the canteen were his guns. They were holstered and clipped to his utility belt. They were Smith and Wesson "Sigma" Series .40 semi-auto pistols. Crack Boy recalled that they were "all over" the target at 15 yards. It was not unusual. The trigger pull on all S & W auto pistols was atrocious. But he knew the same could be said for most double action auto pistols. He'd been told by Mikey J that 500 rounds would have to be shot before the guns bedded in. The triggers were very tight, but he'd bought the guns for defence, not attack. He was no sniper. His neighbourhood was rough, and drive-by shootings were on the up. He needed protection. He had it.

He climbed a gently rising bank and saw that the city was much closer now. The lights from the sprawl were still dim, barely registering. Nothing unusual there.

Why was it sometimes they appeared blindingly bright and at other times so dim? He didn't know. It was not the sparkling razzle of New York or London or Las Vegas. From the window seat of his own private jet he had seen such razzle many times while he toured city to city stadiums. He wondered whether they were candles in the city windows or small gas lamps. Somehow he knew that there was no electricity there. He rubbed the back of his stiff neck, feeling anxious, but not sure why.

He pressed on.

Eager.

Lost in thought, flitting like a butterfly from flower to flower, memory to memory.

He'd once met a pusher on the outskirts of the city, a foul grey, sallow-skinned man, who lived in a broken down shack. It was the closest he'd ever been to the city gates, but once the deal had been done, Crack Boy found himself back hundreds of miles, surrounded by the inevitable swamp lands. The city was a distant sprawl again. He had felt uncontrollably angry and had punched a tree trunk with his stump. He thought that it had bled badly, but he couldn't remember.

The pusher had invited him in to the shack. Like the air itself in the dark world, it stank of soiled odours. The muddy floor was covered in wood shavings, fouled like a hamster's cage. There was a discoloured mattress in one corner of the single room and a twisted, upturned apple box which he used as a table. Tin mugs and plates, stained and unwashed, reminded him of a childhood camping trip to Devon with his biological father, Ken White. He loved the ad-hoc way of life that that week had thrown up. They had been relatively happy days before his eighth birthday.

Now and again, in his more melancholy moments, he longed for those uncomplicated days. The lack of responsibility for anything at all in his childhood was a gift he was unaware of at the time. All of that changed the moment he stepped off the plane onto American soil with his mother and step-father, the big shot navigator, Eddie Steffano.

The pusher sat down heavily on a small, three-legged stool and laid a filthy packet on the box. Crack Boy stood anxiously close to the doorway. There were other things lurking in the shadows that he couldn't quite make out; he didn't wish to stay longer than necessary. He had no desire to sit down.

'Please, take a seat,' the pusher slurred.

'What's your price?' Crack Boy asked, ignoring the offer to sit.

'Three K,' said the pusher, a wry toothless grin creasing his sore lips. He knew the starting bid was extortionate. 'US dollars.'

Crack Boy didn't mind the rip off price. He toyed with the crevice in his chin. Pretending to be deep in thought. He never bartered or haggled. There was no need, because strangely when he took out his wallet, there was always exactly the right amount of cash. If the pusher had asked for Australian dollars or British pounds or Japanese yen, it didn't matter. No problem. Always, he opened his wallet to the exact currency and amount. He didn't think that this was odd, but fortunate. He was used to things like that happening. It was just 'funny drug shit,' he'd said on the few occasions he'd ever spoken to anyone about it.

He handed the money over, taking the small brown packet in return, and muttered something about the son-of-a-bitch cleaning him out. It was all pretence, but it would seem a normal reaction to the deal.

He winced slightly at the sight of the pusher's stained nicotine fingertips. He'd been careful to avoid touching them in the change over.

He'd opened his wallet to show that it was empty for effect. The last thing he wanted was this low life thinking he was loaded. Those dark things that hovered in the shadows of this shack unnerved him. Muggings were commonplace here. Violence was the way people got what they wanted. Although the pusher would have had to deflect the bullets in his Smith and Wesson semi-automatic pistols before getting to within a sniff of his wallet. That wasn't going to happen. He didn't look strong enough. He looked very sick. Stained like the inside of his tin mug – yellowing, grey, and pallid.

Everything changed the instant Crack Boy unfolded the packet, pinched the white powder with his only thumb and index finger into a little mound and snorted.

2

Bang!
Flash!
Light!
Blinding.
Yellowing stains made staccato patterns before his eyes. Patches of light and shade, etched blueprints on his

retina; he suddenly felt an urge to vomit. He threw up, gagging, gasping. Acid licked and rasped the back of his throat. He spat out the remnants of the bile in his mouth. He heaved again and trembled like a gypsy shaking an aspen sapling.

3

He wasn't sure where he was, but he sure as hell knew how he felt. Paranoia was a powerful force. It was in some ways worse that the sweats and shivers and shakes of coming down.

The pusher had ripped him off, no doubt. The packet's contents were bad. Very bad. And something equally as bad had wriggled out of the primordial cortex of his brain, a submerged personality trait, a dark desire. Something shadowy and destructive that he had no power to fight.

He shifted realities now.

The shack had gone, and a dismal hotel room had replaced it. He was living one of his deep-seated desires.

4

Crack Boy peered down at the stain, running as it did like spilled dry coffee or perhaps blood. He knelt down on one clicking knee and sniffed the beige and fawn sofa. It *was* coffee. And more – much more. Disgusting bastards. It smelled faintly of Brazilian blend and foam impregnated with body odours he did not care to consider.

Consider them, you shit!

'Eddie?'

Was that his step-father, Eddie Steffano's voice he had just heard? Surely, it couldn't be.

He gagged at the images resplendent in his mind. Awful, terrible, writhing, pumping, sweating.

No!

He beat his right fingerless hand on the spongy material. His stump. How had he lost his fingers? He couldn't remember. Or perhaps he didn't want to remember.

The sofa responded like a bouncy castle. He pounded it harder. The sound grew louder like the other guests walking with heavy muddy boots above him.

Muffled.

Dull thuds.

More vibration than sound.

Those guests were old and noisy – a bus had off-loaded them at 7pm and they had walked like bleary-eyed sheep into the heart of the hotel. Ba-ba. Old decaying sheep. Or were they ancient vampires out for blood and hell bent on carnage? Random, incoherent thoughts flitted through his blazing mind.

Consider them, you shit! They are old and demand your respect!

'Where are you, Eddie?' Crack Boy said, feeling a slight tickle of fear rising along his spine.

Eddie didn't answer.

There were of course hundreds of fans – much younger – camped outside the hotel, chanting his name. But it wasn't them. They were very loud. This voice was a single voice, not a chanting chorus.

Strange then that he'd gone out onto the balcony which over-looked the crowd and waved, but they hadn't acknowledged him. It was as if he was a ghost, and they couldn't see him.

Half-past dead, Sonny Joe.

Crack Boy twisted his head to where he thought the voice had spoken. But that corner of the room was empty. No Eddie Steffano lurked there. Just shadows, thick and downy. Like the hair on step-father Eddie's chest, he thought, cringing. Of all the images, that one – Eddie's thick downy hairy body – fixed foremost in his mind.

Yes, it had been Eddie's voice, he was certain of that. Only Eddie Steffano called him Sonny Joe. It was his sick joke. Sonny Jim, Sonny Joe. Crack Boy had always detested the nick-name. Bastard knew it, too. He teased him relentlessly when his mother was out.

Crack Boy punched the sofa harder with his fingerless stump. He wished it was Eddie Steffano's head, or Sharkey Jack O'Toole's nose. His hate for both men was unscrambling now. Unseen dust motes entered his mouth and nose. Burning. He pounded the sofa in uncontrolled rage, his eyes stinging with the dust he could now see.

He sneezed. Thousands of droplets of snot sprayed the sofa.

Bang!

Sudden, fleeting illumination.

'You are a ghost, you dumb arse,' he snarled. 'That's why they couldn't see you!'

He smiled crazily and his eyes wrinkled. He sniffed. A habit. Bad habit, but he was clean now for over a week. Rehab was a good thing, his social worker told him. She was right. She was blonde. She was out of order wearing those tight sweaters.

What the fuck was he talking about? Out of rehab for over a week? How did he know that? He couldn't. He was dead, wasn't he?

But it seemed like a week ago. He was so confused. Time was so hard to gauge in this…this other place he inhabited. It was a dismal hazy place, and yet at other times it was cut-throat sharp. It was as real as any place he'd been to. But he did not feel comforted by the fact. He was dead. He'd seen the bastard who'd murdered him. But the albino wasn't the only one.

There had been more. There had been a plan, and an intent to kill him. He knew them well. They would pay. Oh, how they would pay. O'Toole had been behind the murder. He'd hired the albino to assassinate him. Yes, that's what he'd done.

'Now that doesn't make sense, Sonny Joe,' he heard a familiar voice but saw no-one. 'And you know it. Let go of your paranoid delusions. You are a coke-head, Crack Boy. Face the fact. You are useless, Sonny Joe. You are a waste of space. You know what the USAF would do to a jerk like you? Don't you? Discipline! That's right. Good old fashioned, short, sharp, shock discipline.'

He turned, twisted. 'Who's there?'

Silence.

No-one in the room.

The voice was right.

It didn't make sense. A single silver dollar? That was not the weapon of an assassin. An assassin would have waited high on a roof top somewhere, sniper's rifle and telescopic sights aimed at his heart.

Bang!

End of story.

He pounded across the blue carpet and stood in the threshold of the toilet. He was naked. And stiff. His flesh crawled with goose bumps.

He shivered.

He sniffed.

Fluorescent yellow light pulsed, flickered, reflected dim light against the mirror. In spite of the oppressive humidity of the swamps, he shivered a lot in this dark world. But he felt colder than usual. Why was that?

Next door Jack snored in a 3 a.m. rhythm. Jack was alive – just. Oh Jacky boy, he thought. Oh Jacky boy, I've got a sick surprise for you.

Jack O'Toole was an arsehole of a manager. He'd arranged gigs, negotiated record and publishing deals and coordinated tours for Crack Boy, and he'd skimmed the cream. Why did O'Toole give Steffano, the pathetic 'twin kid,' all of Crack Boy's earnings? He was a rat of a man, a black-hearted and money pinching bastard. He'd screwed Crack Boy's bank balance hard. He screwed all his acts hard. He'd kept two sets of accounts – one for his clients and the taxman and another for himself.

And what had Joey Steffano done to stop Sharkey O'Toole?

Nothing.

Sweet FA.

In all likelihood he was behind the scam.

Some time passed, but Crack Boy wasn't sure how much. He wouldn't look at his watch. The glass was shattered like a spider's web. He hated it. But he wouldn't take it off. Ever. It had been his mother's watch. She had big wrists and tattoos on her shoulders. She had worn Nike trainers and JJB joggers. She had smoked forty a day. She had snorted coke with the worst of them. She had died laughing in his arms, watching Homer and Bart outrun a pink dinosaur, a smoking cigarette hanging limply in her yellow-tipped fingers.

The doctor was a twat. He'd said she'd died of an asthma attack brought on by smoking and laughing and coughing and choking. Her coke-smoking habit hadn't helped much either. The snorting had compounded matters.

'So tell me something I don't know,' Crack Boy muttered to his mirror image.

Crack Boy still loved the Simpsons, but he hated pink dinosaurs. His mind was wandering incoherently. He remembered flicking cable channels on his remote control.

'Animal studies have shown that animals will work very hard (press a bar over 10,000 times) for a single injection of cocaine, choose cocaine over food and water, and take cocaine even when this behaviour is punished.'

He thought about his own addiction. He craved the highs as much as the animals. He was a hopeless cause, he knew. But he didn't care anymore. Everything was pointless in the long run. Death would smash you hard when you least expected it, so what was the point of low-fat diets and carbohydrate watching? We all ended up dead, whichever way you lived your life.

'Death isn't the Grim-Reaper carrying a sickle and a skeletal grimace. Death's a sudden car crash or an insane suicide bomb or a devastating tsunami. Death comes to most of us when you least expect it.'

Bang!

Thoughts came and left like lovers and their offspring. He thought about Daisy's tits and Jane's arse, and Lyla's long slim waist, and Uncle Frank's shaven pins. He imagined them joined together to form the perfect fantasy.

But the dark thought of Eddie's matted chest haunted him. He spoke out to Eddie, challenging him to step out of the shadows, but he was gutless. He didn't appear. Didn't utter a word, even.

He wasn't such a big man now that Crack Boy was all grown up. I owe you, Eddie Steffano. You ain't gonna beat me any more. I'm the one who's gonna be doing all the beating from now on.

Time passed, his thoughts formed and unformed like a fluid Rubik's cube.

Snap.

Thought became feeling, became the dim reality of the hotel room. Yes, reality must win, he thought.

For now.

Crack Boy knew it was time to leave. He ceased pounding his bruised head against the toilet wall. The fucking light was driving him mad. It buzzed intermittently, flickered now and again. He wished it would stop, or go, or blow the fuck up.

He glanced at his haggard, fifty year old face in the mirror. What's wrong with me? Why do I look so old? I'm nineteen, not ninety! Why so old?

He touched the mirror. Perhaps something was wrong with it. Perhaps it was like that weird holographic shit he'd seen in *Star Trek*. But how could it reflect such an ancient thing?

His stubble was rising from his cleft chin. His pale skin looked almost tanned in this light. Almost. He flirted with thoughts of beaches and fast red cars and neon strip lighting in shady humid alleyways in exotic places. Bangkok, Bombay, Hong Kong. Steamy windows filled with pert, bronzed naked flesh.

He bent down and grabbed his discarded black shoe by its scuffed toe. He crashed the heel down against the light with all the strength he possessed. The light splintered into a myriad of tiny shards. Popping.

Darkness flooded the room, except for the TV. Dark, darker, darkest.

He liked the dark, the half light. Bright lights made his eyes hurt.

Half-past dead.

He ignored the chicken in the shadows.

He shook glass from his shaggy black hair. Where had that come from? It wasn't there a moment ago, was it? His hair was short and peroxide. Strange. How could his hair change colour and grow so long in such a short space of time?

He knew that his face had been cut in several places, like a razor-happy freak. But his eyes were fine. The dark Joey Ramone shades had shielded him. Had they been perched on his nose before? He couldn't remember. Did it matter?

Probably not.

And he noticed something else about his face. His upper lip was cut. He could feel the metallic-sweet blood as he flicked the tip of his tongue onto his moist lips. Stinging.

Crack Boy barely noticed the music – a waltz or hip-hop beat – in the distance from the party in the conference room. That room was full of musicians, journalists, record company executives, publishers, fans. That arse Joey Steffano was in there accepting another award on behalf of Crack Boy, who was 'unavoidably disposed, and temporarily unavailable.' He could just hear the two-faced little shit, expounding his hip-hop-rock virtues to the masses. There would be a live satellite link to MTV or ABC or some big-shot network. Billions would see the awards most likely. It made Crack Boy want to puke. Why did so many people think Joey Steffano was so goddamn cool?

He walked over to the double bed and sat down on the edge of it.

'I know what you are up to, Steffano,' Crack Boy muttered. 'You've been trying to off-load me for sometime now. You used me on that last album, and now you want to reinvent yourself again. But I ain't moving over, Steffano. Crack Boy likes the hip-hop superstar life. It's gonna take more of a man than you to kick my arse!'

That award room needed a stick of dynamite tossing into it. Lock all the doors. Turn out the lights. Blow the egotistical, posing arseholes to smithereens.

Yes!

With all those awards and prizes that room would burn like hell on bonfire night. Up in smoke! Up in flames!

Yes!

No.

Crack Boy was more subtle, more secretive than that. He felt a swell of pride rise in his groin. Stiff, ready, alive.

Mister Subtle, that's me.

Crack Boy the fucking Budgie.

Cute, blue, twittering.

Caged.

Perched, eager to peck the eyeballs from any fucker willing to let me! Cute, but wild and unpredictable.

He sprang to his feet and shoved his fingerless hand into his mouth. He turned slowly, paused and gazed absently at the T.V. screen. *Adult movies – non-stop British adult movies available 24 hours a day, movies – Harry Potter, Playstation, play all games for £2.00 per hour!*

Rip off!

He read the yellow and black message at the bottom of the screen. 'Charging is automatic upon starting each channel, movies will appear as *Room Service* on your bill.'

Not today.

Rip off!

He leaned and picked up the Playstation controller with his good scarred three-fingered hand. How many people? he wondered. How many sweaty beer-stained hands had mauled the controller?

Who were these people?

Where were they now?

Leading normal lives in an abnormal society? City bound, or rural? Male or female? Transsexual or gay? Anonymous co-inhabitants of the one night stand room. He tethered his imagination.

Heel, boy.

Come to boot!

He dropped it. The controller bounced on the blue carpet.

He twisted, lurching towards the yellow stained wall. The banal floral pattern seemed beautiful. Now that was ridiculous. He knew he was tripping, but that self-awareness was a fleeting thing, quickly lost.

Now was the time, the moment had arrived. Action stations, Crack Boy.

Go get him!

He kicked out a shoeless naked foot.

5

He slipped from his room into Jack's room as if a leaf falling from an ash tree in autumn. The space between the fall and the ground ceased to exist. The transition from one room to the next was seamless. He was no longer physical, even though he could feel. He travelled what some might consider time and space. He had been dead for how long?

Days?

Weeks?

Months?

He wasn't sure.

It didn't matter anymore.

He was in control now.

He stood next to snoring Jack and his face split with a grin. He fingered the crevice in his chin. He breathed silently through his nose, the odd whistle of nose hair faintly puncturing Jack's open snoring maw.

He saw Jack's face changing in the dim light. First it

was Joey's smug face and then it transformed into hard-nose Eddie Steffano. Hatred of all three of them welled up in his chest, made it difficult to breathe or swallow. These three faces came and went, spinning like slowly revolving doors.

Death comes in the dead of night, Crack Boy thought. He could have known Jack all his life, but the few years he'd been manager was enough. The old senile sod had cut some impressive deals, but what had happened to all those millions?

Ripped off.

But not anymore. It would be so easy, he thought. So easy to take him out. Let him join me here in this dark world of illusion. Then we'll see how he copes.

Later.

You have no idea what your filthy stealing hands will cost you, O'Toole. And you, my bad step-father, you will pay for those beatings and humiliation. And the 'twin kid?'

He'd get all he deserved. Pathetic, weak-willed loser.

Streaked light dappled the old man's wrinkled features. The creature that was Crack Boy loomed over him, more ancient and ruined than ever. Hatred plastered a grotesque mask over his youth.

Arcane. Dark, abysmal thoughts formed like dyslexia in his mind.

Crack Boy took out his stump from his mouth. It really was a stump, severed at the wrist, new skin covered it like pink tarpaulin. His mind flamed with fire images. He couldn't remember how the stump had appeared instead of a hand and fingers. But there was something that…

No. A shield before his eyes. Bad memories blanked for his own sanity. Yes, that was it. Blanked for his sanity.

He bit deeper and harder. His hand dripped blood where he'd punctured the flesh with his broken polished teeth.

He moved his stump so that the droplets of blood dripped into Jack's open mouth. Tiny drops hit the old man's tongue. Some splattered his gums. Some dripped onto his upper lip and trickled down the old man's wrinkled chin.

Crack Boy looked at the bedside cabinet. There was a glass, chipped on its lip. Inside, the false teeth were surrounded by tiny bubbles, immersed in Sterodent and water.

False.

Old.

Teeth.

The only light in the room came from the T.V. screen. Yellow. It was enough.

He blinked.

He breathed slowly, wondering how much blood would fall into the old man's maw before he awoke or choked.

Dripping.

Snoring.

Crack Boy waited.

The waiting was everything. The guessing what would happen next.

Muddy old, heavy feet disco-danced above him. Raised laughter, clinking glasses, babbled conversation.

Blood dripping.

I am here, a fiction in the telling. You are there, talking it up in the way only singers and writers can. I am here. Dripping, slowly dripping my life force, my young blood into the old dying man's maw.

Dripping, slowly, dripping.

Slowly.

Staining the neck of his starched white collar. Choking like mother, coughing like her, too. But not laughing.

No.

Only mother could die laughing.

Smoking, watching Homer.

6

Crack Boy shook the trip from his head like a dog shaking water from its fur after a swim in the ocean. He was breathing heavily, as he'd run miles in his head. He was back at the swamp, looking up at the sign that pointed toward the city sprawl.

Journey's End – The Ultimate High.

He sat down and allowed himself a mouthful of vodka from the canteen. He thought of Jack O'Toole's gagging mouth and wondered if he'd actually killed him or was it just another crazy episode induced by drugs?

He wasn't sure, which unsettled him.

Real or illusion?

The question was worrying, but since there was no obvious answer, he tossed it aside.

All of the hatred he had felt for Joey and steady Eddie Steffano and Jack O'Toole had subsided somewhat, too. It was now like a dull toothache, instead of a throbbing fire of non-stop pain.

He scanned the dark world and then looked up at the city, which was now shimmering like a far-away mirage, a distant crown of jewels that was always just out of reach.

There was something else shimmering on the horizon, a ball of light, which unnerved him. He wasn't sure why. Perhaps it was the intensity of that globe of light. So much dark here, then…a light?

It didn't make sense.

He got up, feeling the first pangs of hunger. Soon that incredible thirst would arrive, and he knew that he would do anything, do whatever it took to quench it.

He must get to the city.

There would be clean water there.

He hitched up his utility belt, replacing his canteen. He trudged along the Yellow Brick Road toward his goal like a dark shadow of Frankenstein's monster.

Chapter Four

Crazy Talk

1

Joey got up on unsteady legs and hurried along the aisle. He was trembling, like the after effects of GHB. It had all happened so fast and was over in a flash. He stopped at the back of the carriage and looked at the dark hole.

He peered deeply into it, but couldn't see a falling creature. He'd expected to see something – a flash of colour or a splash of reflected light on the creature's body. But there was nothing there except the void.

But he was sure he'd seen something as the creature had leapt into the void. For a split second he'd seen *something*. Sparks maybe? But he couldn't quite conjure the image from his mind to be definite.

A crazy part of Joey wanted to put his hand through the hole. But he was trembling with fear from the attack, and now very anxious about the dark chasm. Perhaps it was an illusion. It didn't make any sense whatsoever that the creature should dive into that pool of blackness like a suicide bomber intent on a mission with no compromise. But the creature had jumped, silently, launching itself as if its fall would be broken.

By what?

A trampoline?

A mattress?

An ocean?

He didn't know. He felt that he was clutching crumbling straw. But he just had to know what was out there. What would he find if he launched himself into the abyss?

He crouched down on his haunches just a few feet from the void, rocking back and forth on the heel and sole of his trainers. He had to think this through – carefully.

What should he do next?

At least he was alone here. Annie and Harry and Ellen and all the rest were back there somewhere. Think more. Play around with a few ideas in the hope that one of them might actually make some sense.

He came back to one central theme: illusion. Was what he saw really there? That was the main question he had to find out. He wasn't prepared to take the risk himself; not just yet. He was in no immediate danger. But what if the crazy thing returned? What if other things came out of him, like the predators he'd been warned about who picked up the scent of a soul like wolves pick up the scent of blood miles away?

Then what?

Then he'd have to either fight or take a chance and run and jump through the ripped carriage into the deep black hole of space.

He itched the cleft of his chin, mulling. Was it really deep space out there? He squinted his eyes and strained to find a point of light, a star, a planet reflecting a nearby sun's radiance. But no, nothing. Deep blackness, almost velvety, like a curtain.

He laughed.

So absurd.

Who'd he think was hiding behind that piece of fabric? The fucking Wizard of Oz?

'Are you okay?' Annie said. She had ventured as far as the entrance of the half carriage, but seemed reluctant to step closer.

'Yes, thanks,' he said.

In spite of his best judgement, he still felt attracted to Annie. She was crazy, yes. But perhaps it would be foolish to dismiss her totally. She might prove to be useful. Indeed, she had been *more* than useful – she'd probably saved him from a hell of a beating.

'I'm just trying to figure something out.' He looked up at her and smiled awkwardly. 'Can you leave me here awhile?'

'Sure. I understand,' she said, and returned to her seat.

I doubt it, Joey thought and returned to his own thoughts.

He slipped back a few moments in his mind. It had all happened so fast and was over in a flash. What had the creature looked like as it melted from the carriage into the black hole? Had it simply vanished? One moment here, and the next gone? Or had it melted like butter reducing in a hot pan, from solid to something akin to a liquid state? Or perhaps it had faded, like a shadow when the sun exposed itself from behind a bank of clouds? He couldn't focus long enough in his memory to prise open a definite answer. But he felt that it was crucial if he were to move forward in his understanding. The way something moves from one moment to another is important, he told himself. But he wasn't sure why.

81

He gazed absently at the filthy floor and saw strewn beneath the seats some empty Coke and Pepsi cans, cardboard Costa Rica coffee cups, crisp packets, sweet wrappers, discarded plastic sandwich cartons. And in an instant he saw a way forward, a flash of inspiration.

He also saw the price sticker on the sandwich carton and felt more confused to his location than ever. The carton had held a bacon and egg granary sandwich which had cost £1.99.

This is a British Rail train, he thought. How the hell can that be? But it made sense of the landscape he'd seen. That was typically English. But he'd been performing on stage, hadn't he? In New York?

He shook his head. He couldn't recall everything clearly. Was it New York or Texas? There were snatches of images – something silver, crowds cheering or screaming, a pulsing rhythm, stage lights, hot and blinding, then…

It was too much. Small beads of sweat were appearing on his forehead from the mental effort. The chronological events leading up to his conscious awareness of the train journey were scrambled and incomplete.

Annoyingly so; but he held out a small light of hope: he remembered more now – however scrambled – than he had half an hour ago. Perhaps his memory was returning? Perhaps the Snakehead drug cocktail was wearing off?

Joey Steffano rocked onto his knees and stretched out his hand. He grabbed a Coke can and held it before him like a trophy. He felt a small ripple of elation ride through him.

It was worth a try.

*

2

Joey stood up and raised the Coke can above his head. When it hit the void, he'd have his chance to glimpse what was hidden beyond. He was sure there was something, but not so sure what. He had ideas – a light-filled landscape, a shimmering blue ocean, a catwalk to another world. Wishful thinking, of course, for he'd only glimpsed a fraction of a second. But he had to know; and more importantly he had to get off the train.

He drew his right arm back further and instinctively raised his left arm up in front of him. He covered his face.

He launched the can at the void with all the strength he possessed. It shimmied through the air, spinning over and over. It struck the blackness and vanished in silence. There were no sparks, no flash of light to illuminate a hidden world – just blackness. One moment it was in the carriage, and the next it was not.

'Shit,' Joey grumbled. It hadn't reacted how he'd expected.

He sat down heavily in the nearest seat. His head was throbbing where the silver dollar protruded. He lightly touched the flesh around it. It was sore, and probably infected. I need to get something for it. TCP or medicine or something. He wasn't sure what exactly – just that it needed some attention before it got worse. Perhaps guardian Franklin was a first-aid guy, or there might be a doctor onboard. If Annie was to be believed then you'd expect the train to be crawling with medical staff, stitching up the newly dead and their fatal wounds.

He chuckled at the absurdity of the notion.

He refocused on the black hole.

'It changes,' he said, his voice tinged with frustration and a little disappointment.

He looked at the void. It changed, he thought. First sparks, now nothing. Perhaps I was mistaken. No sparks at all. Nothing but an abyss. Or perhaps living things reacted differently with the void.

He thought for a moment. What did he have on him heavy enough to make a real impact? Surprisingly very little that he was prepared to part with. His car keys, his mobile and his knife. That was it. Not even I.D. or credit cards or cash. He never took them on stage with him, but he couldn't bear to part with his keys, mobile and knife. One thing was certain: he wouldn't be throwing any of those treasures into the void in the name of science.

He thought some more.

Minutes passed, and then wham! There it was before his eyes. It wasn't major league Einstein stuff, but it would have to do.

In a rush of eagerness, he jumped up off the seat and scrambled around beneath it. He scooped out the debris. He knocked aside the lightweight plastic sandwich carton. It was too flimsy. He fingered the cardboard coffee cup. Not heavy enough. He placed a Pepsi can inside it, ramming and twisting to form a tight bond. He was determined to try again. If he was right, then he expected no reaction, no sparks from the inanimate objects he now raised above his head.

He hurled the coffee cup stuffed with a Pepsi can as hard as he could at the hole. The darkness swallowed it. No sparks, no light.

He tried another can but the result was the same.

Unless another creature obliged by emerging from his naval and leaping into the void, then Joey Steffano wouldn't know for certain what lay hidden beyond. Still, he was a little wiser for his experiment, and the train was a little cleaner.

He wondered what he should do next. He had two choices, as far as he could see. Either he could remain where he was with Annie and the zombies; wait for the train to take him to Journey's End. Or he could explore more carriages. He didn't like the prospect of either. The waiting would drive him nuts. He had to take some control; or *feel* that he was taking control at least. Take control and feel less stressed.

Good advice.

Wise words.

He turned and strode along the aisle toward the carriages further ahead. He had a bad feeling about this.

Very bad.

3

The carriage ahead was empty. Annie, everyone there had gone. Where? He didn't know. Perhaps they had moved further up, out of his way after his outburst and the terrifying incident with the creature. What had Annie called it?

His dark half or something.

Crazy.

The next carriage was empty, too. Harry and Ellen were nowhere to be seen.

As he reached the adjoining carriage, the train lurched violently, shuddered. Joey thought that they had hit something on the track.

He grabbed a head-rest and instinctively covered his head in the crook of his free arm. He dropped to his knees, both hands covering the top of his head, burying his face in the springy velvet of a train seat.

Bang!

The explosion lit up the horizon like a bolt of sheet lightning. A great yellow-white flash was followed a split second later by an almighty boom, boom, boom. A dark pillar of smoke rose high into the air, mushrooming at the top.

The train juddered on the rails and sparks flew from the wheels.

Joey glanced behind him and gasped. Either the carriage had been ripped in half again, or the dark hole had gobbled up the carriages at the rear of the train. Whatever the cause, the result was terrifyingly clear: another dark hole (or perhaps it was the same dark hole?) was less than fifteen feet from Joey. Jagged metal teeth encircled the chasm where the carriage had been severed.

He briefly wondered if the two incidents were related in some way – the explosion and the advancement of the black hole.

He got up quickly and hurried toward the carriage ahead of him. His head was pounding where the coin stuck out. The redness around it was getting worse. Yellow pus wept from the top of the wound.

He needed a doctor – fast.

*

4

As Joey entered the next carriage he noticed that it was empty except for the *Rolling Stone* reader. The old bald guy was sitting by the window, reading the *New York Times*. He poked the headline with his long bony finger.

'Seen this, superstar? Seen what's happening out there?' He nodded toward the window, where a column of black smoke rose. 'It ain't good, son. No, sir. It ain't a pretty sight.'

'Was that an explosion?'

'Yep. Spot on, son. Hope for you yet.' He let a wry grin curl his lips for a moment, then his relaxed face tightened. 'Gotta hurry. More folk to pick up.'

Joey edged closer and sat down opposite the man. Hurry? More folk to pick up?

'I know what you're thinking, son. You don't have to be a mind-reader. It's plainer than day – right there on your face.' He held out a rough hand. 'Name's Franklin,' he said. 'Franklin J Merryhill.'

Joey took the man's cold hand and shook it hard. His grip of steel was met by an equal grip of steel. One thing his dad taught him as a small kid: *you can tell the stuff of a man by the type of handshake he delivers.* He was tempted to tell him that he already knew his name – had always known his name most probably – but he kept it to himself. It was just another oddity to add to a growing list of idiosyncrasies he'd experienced onboard the train to Journey's End.

'Who are we picking up?'

'Folk out there.' Franklin nodded toward the smoke.

'They'll be wandering right now. Lost. Confused. Dead. We need to hurry.'

Joey raised an inquisitive eyebrow.

'Gotta get them all aboard for the journey to the end of the line, son. I told you that already? End of the line? The place we're heading? Told you that, too – right? Memory's not what it used to be, son.' He scratched his forehead. 'Or perhaps it was those other new folk back there I told?'

Joey shrugged. 'Whatever. But you're full of it, mister. You told me I was dead, but that's bullshit. You and Annie and those other two dumb wits are scamming me. That's it, isn't it?'

Franklin smiled, flashing white teeth. 'You reckon, son?'

Joey ignored the ironic tone. He was certain. 'But there's another problem – one that's more pressing.'

Franklin followed Joey's anxious gaze toward the end of the carriage. 'The black hole.'

'Yes. As you know so much about this train journey, I'm sure you can tell me – what the hell is that thing?'

'What do you think it is superstar?'

'If I knew I wouldn't be asking.'

'But you got ideas, son. Haven't you?'

Joey had ideas but he wasn't going to share them with this arsehole. 'Cut the mind game crap, mister, and tell me what you know.'

'It doesn't work that way onboard this train, son. You ain't Starsky or Hutch. You don't give out the orders, Captain Ahab. You have no authority here. All of your money and fame and influence over the millions of fans who loved to groove to your music when you were alive, that don't count for a thing here, boy. You only have yourself, son.'

Franklin's tone was level and cool, not a hint of malice, but lots of calm authority, like someone who knows they have the advantage simply because they know the terrain, know the rules of the game. It was true also – Joey only had himself, and a little more besides. There was his broken mobile, his car keys and his knife. He felt strangely reassured by the idea of his knife.

A stabbing pain ripped through his temple and he became acutely aware of the protruding coin. He reached up and touched the redness around it. It smarted like hell now.

'Looks like you need a medic, son.' Franklin smiled, and leaned forward. His hand snaked out toward Joey's head. 'You want me to take a look at that for you?'

Joey recoiled at the sight of Franklin's fingertips. They seemed to glow momentarily with white light.

'I'm all right,' he said, blinking.

Franklin withdrew his hand and his fingers returned to their usual colour.

Joey sat silently for awhile, trying to think through what he'd seen in a rational manner. Trick of the light, he told himself. There are always flashes of light from outside trains. Windows are made of glass, right? Glass reflects all kinds of light sources. That was it – a reflection.

But as he gazed at the changing landscape, he hadn't completely convinced himself. Franklin's fingers had glowed – actually glowed. Perhaps he's a magician. Yes! That was it. Magicians can perform all kinds of weird illusions – Blaine, Copperfield, Houdini.

Magic.

Illusion.

Nothing more than sleight of hand.

A glowing hand?

Illusion.

He thought some more, attempted to jerk himself back to the here and now. He formulated his next question and spoke.

'How *does* it work here?' Joey said, laying off the tantrum. It was probably not wise to mess with this guy. He probably had all kinds of tricks up his sleeve. He stifled laughter.

'Manners make a man, don't they? *Please* and *thank you* are great words. They open up so many doors. Like magic keys.'

'What did you say?'

'You heard me, son. Now pay attention, please.'

Magic keys? He read my mind. Why did he pick out *that* word of all the words he could have chosen? Magic key and magic fingers? He's fooling with me. He's playing mind games. Perhaps he's a stage hypnotist? Perhaps he is-

Stop it! he scolded himself. *You'll have him down for the Sugar Plum Fairy next or freakin' Santa Claus. This theorising will just screw up your head, man.* And he knew that wasn't hard to do.

'A little respect for your elders. A little looser and lighter? What do you think superstar? Is it cool to chill?'

Joey was certain now that the guy was playing sad mind games, but he wouldn't tell him. He thought that he was already at enough of a disadvantage, without adding further distress to a miserable situation.

'I'm sorry,' he said. 'I'm a little stressed. All I want is to get off this train and go home.'

'I know, son. I know.'

There was a real sadness in Franklin's voice right then. Perhaps that's the way forward, the way out of this mess, Joey thought. Give the old guy what he wants. Play along with his game. Break down the barriers and learn; wait and be patient. That's how he'd eventually come to lead The Breakers. He'd been patient; he'd adapted; changed his attitude and accent. If needs be, he'd change again. If nothing else he was a survivor, an opportunist.

The chance to get off this train will appear again, he told himself. Save your energy for the break out. Play it light. Loosen up as the old feller wants. Chill and stay cool. But that was easier to think than do.

Outside, pin-pricks of light flickered from distant horizon cities, yellow and sallow yet resplendent. A dirty smog was spewing out from tall brick chimneys and there came a sense of overwhelm, a sense of scurrilous drizzle that was emaciated with immortal misery and filthy frailty. Somewhere out there something scuttled amidst the dank alleys and back streets, illuminating the radiance not of love and kindness but of hatred and malice. Joey felt it deep inside his heart. Something pretending to be the light was stalking him, but he could not pin-point its source. It was an invisible something, far darker than anything sentient had a right to be. It moved fast, feeding from the inner light of others. It was a spiritual leech, a parasite of the heart, a sucker of the intellect. He wasn't certain how he knew this, yet somehow Joey's internal narrator communicated the knowledge to him. Somehow. But was it nothing more than a paranoid emotion, a vulnerability built on the weirdness of his journey?

Perhaps. He didn't know; couldn't know.

After a few moments silence, Joey spoke. 'What was that explosion?'

Franklin tapped the headline again. 'Hot off the press, son. Take a look – see? But that's only the half of it. It's a busy day. We've a lot of pick ups. Lord only knows where we are gonna get the time.'

Election Fears Over New Suicide Bombers' Attack

Suicide car bombers have struck Iraq's two main Shi'ite holy cities of Najaf and Kerbala, killing at least 92 people and wounding nearly 170, six weeks before a second historic election.

Both bombs, which went off about three hours apart on Monday, exploded near crowded bus stations in a seemingly synchronized attempt to cause as much bloodshed as possible among Shi'ites, a long-oppressed majority expected to dominate the January 30th vote.

Earlier in Baghdad, gunmen killed three Electoral Commission employees after hauling them from a car on a busy street.

The bomb blasts were not far from important shrines – the Imam Ali mosque in Najaf and Imam Hussein mosque in Kerbala.

The attacks seemed designed to provoke sectarian disagreement with Saddam Hussein's long-dominant Sunni minority – officials have seen similar motives behind previous attacks in the cities.

Shi'ite leaders called on their people not to reply in kind.

In Najaf, the suicide bomber detonated his vehicle about 300 yards from the Imam Ali shrine, near crowds of people queuing for buses and taxis and not far from busy offices.

Medical officials said there were at least 56 dead and 80 wounded in the blast, which left stunned crowds waiting in freezing temperatures for ambulances. A thick column of smoke rose from the blast site as a rare drizzling rain fell.

Police applied a curfew in Najaf's old city.

In Kerbala, where a suicide bomber hit about three hours earlier, the main hospital said 17 people were killed and 45 wounded. A hospital official said all appeared to be civilians with many women and children amongst them.

A cameraman for Reuters who filmed the aftermath of the attack said the ground around the bus station was littered with dead and wounded. Flames licked at the burnt-out vehicles nearly an hour afterwards.

The explosion left a deep crater and blew out windows and shop fronts, showering the area with broken glass.

(Remit: 42 suicide bomb victims still unaccounted for. Keep searching entry point B73, Sector Middle East).

5

Joey's pretence of loose and light didn't last long. The old guy was having a laugh at Joey's expense. 'What are you telling me? Do you think I'm stupid?'

'You said it, son. Yes, sir. You sure did.'

Joey waved at the billowing smoke, much closer than he might have thought possible. The train was really moving fast now. Like one of those bullet trains, only impossibly faster. Blue sparks flew off the wheels as they juddered around a bend.

'Do you think I'm going to believe your crap about picking up the dead on this ghost train?'

'Believe what you want, superstar. It ain't gonna change a thing. You dead, boy. Them poor folk out there are dead, too. Just doing my job, son. Can you understand that?'

Joey thought about what Annie had told him – that this train was picking up the dead and that Franklin was the boss.

'What *is* your job?' Joey said.

'Dead collector, soul saver, kind benevolent bald guy.' He raised his hand in a sweeping motion. He chopped the air like Blair or Bush as he made his points. 'That's me – Franklin J Merryhill. Rescuer of the dead.'

Joey fought a smile. More bull, he thought. This guy isn't a magician or a hypnotist. This guy is a circus clown – no, a circus ringmaster!

'I run this train because no-one else will, or can, son,' he said without bragging. 'It has to be done.'

'Why?'

'If you spent some time out there in that wilderness all alone, then you'd understand. When I first passed over, I wasn't as fortunate as you, son. No, sir. I know what it's like because I managed to survive out there for awhile until this train came by and the good folk onboard rescued me. Now they'd been working on here for a long time, and them folks deserved a break, son. They had family of their own to catch up with. So they taught me the ropes and I took over the reins. You understand where I'm coming from? Eternally grateful – that's what I'll always be.'

Franklin shook his head reflectively, and for the first time Joey saw his face etched with terror. 'The entities out there that feed on the dead are dark souls. Believe me, son. It's an awful place to be.'

'Yeah, I know,' Joey said. 'You told me that little gem before.'

'And I'll no doubt tell you again. It's worth remembering what an awful place it is with no friends, no one who cares about you. Being hunted is a terrible thing, son. You run and run, hiding here and there, but eventually those demons catch up with you. Then they drain you of every good thought in your head. They steal all the light from your mind. After that, you have no choice but to become one of them – greedy, evil, selfish. Unless of course…'

'This train gets to you first and picks you up,' Joey said, sighing. 'I get the picture. I don't need any more lectures.'

'Fine by me, son. My advice is free. No small print. No fee to pay. But if you don't want to take it, then that's your concern.'

'You sound like you are lecturing me again.'

'Sorry, son. Force of habit, I guess. It's the teenagers that I have the most difficulty with – convincing them that they are dead to the old world. Stubborn as hell, that's what they are.'

Joey huffed and slouched in the seat. Why wouldn't this guy shut up? This had to be a dream. One of those long vivid dreams you get now and again when you're all stressed and strung out or something. And what camel crap – picking up the dead from a suicide bomb attack.

He looked at the column beneath the headline story. He didn't want to read it, but it was better than listening to the old guy's crazy talk.

Tsunami Death Toll Rises To 160,000

Banda Aceh, Indonesia (Reuters) – Thousands of corpses are rotting in Indonesia's tropical sun, as rescuers scour remote coastlines across the Indian Ocean for survivors of Sunday's giant waves that killed more than 160,000.

Many who escaped death in what may have been the deadliest tsunami in more than 200 years now face a fight for survival against hunger and disease. The United Nations mobilised what it called the biggest relief operation in its history.

The ocean surge was triggered by a 9.0-magnitude undersea earthquake, the biggest in 40 years, off the Indonesian island of Sumatra, spreading in an arc of death across the Indian Ocean and striking from Indonesia to Sri Lanka, and beyond to Africa.

U.S. scientists said the quake that set off the killer wall of water permanently moved tectonic plates beneath the Indian Ocean as much as 30 metres, slightly shifting islands near Sumatra. It may also have made the Earth wobble on its axis.

Survivors told harrowing tales of the moment the tsunami, up to 10 metres high, struck towns and resorts, sucking holidaymakers off beaches into the ocean and smashing people and debris through buildings.

UNICEF executive director Carol Bellamy said children could account for up to a third of the dead.

Indonesia has suffered the biggest number of victims, with 62,502 known to be dead and a final toll of 80,000 expected.

President Susilo Bambang Yudhoyono spoke of "frightening reports" from outlying parts of Aceh province, on the northern tip of Sumatra and closest to the quake's epicentre.

The stench of decomposing corpses spread over the provincial capital, Banda Aceh, and fresh water, food and fuel were running short. Many in the city feared fresh quakes and tsunamis, and roads were filled with people trying to leave.

"There is no food here whatsoever. We need rice. We need petrol. We need medicine. I haven't eaten in two days," said Vaiti Usman, a woman in her mid-30s, gesturing angrily at her filthy sarong, saying it was the last of her possessions.

Soldiers and volunteers were collecting corpses scattered on the streets for mass burial.

AID TEAMS ARRIVE

International aid teams landed in devastated villages as health experts said disease could kill as many people as the waves.

The World Food Programme was sending trucks of food to parts of Sri Lanka while the Red Cross despatched sanitation teams to villages in Sri Lanka and Indonesia.

Munich Re, the world's largest reinsurer, estimated the economic cost of the devastation at more than $13 billion (6.7 billion pounds). Indonesia said the cost of rebuilding Sumatra would be $1 billion.

U.S. Secretary of State Colin Powell said the international community may have to give billions of dollars in aid.

The United States more than doubled its pledge to $35 million and ordered 12 vessels, including the aircraft carrier

USS Abraham Lincoln, to the region.

Australia increased its aid to $27 million and said it, the United States, Japan and India were considering setting up a core group to coordinate help.

"A lot of the economies, or sectors of the economies, of the affected countries have been close to being destroyed and it is going to require a great deal of rebuilding and a great deal of investment," said Australian Foreign Minister Alexander Downer.

SURVIVING ON COCONUTS

In Sri Lanka, where the death toll neared 42,000, Tamil Tiger rebels in the north appealed for help as they dug mass graves to bury thousands of bodies. All 135 children at an orphanage run by women rebels were killed.

Rescue teams headed out to the last of India's remote Andaman and Nicobar islands that have been cut off since Sunday. People on some of the isles have been surviving on coconuts.

India's overall toll of nearly 24,500 included at least 14,000 killed on the islands, which are closer to Myanmar and Indonesia than to the Indian mainland. On one, the surge of water killed two-thirds of the population.

"One in every five inhabitants in the entire Nicobar group of islands is either dead, injured or missing," a police official said. Dozens of aftershocks above 5.0 on the Richter scale have rocked the islands.

In parts of India's Tamil Nadu state officials gave up trying to count the dead and were counting survivors instead, while burying bodies as quickly as possible in mass graves.

In Thailand, where thousands of tourists had been enjoying a peak-season Christmas break to escape the northern winter, many west-coast resorts were turned into graveyards.

The government said that, of its toll of more than 1,500 dead, 473 were known to be foreigners, among them 54 Swedes, 49 Germans, 43 Britons and 84 identified only as Caucasian.

Rescue workers had recovered 1,200 bodies at Khao Lak beach, north of Phuket island, and more than 300 had been found on remote Phi Phi island, made famous in the film "The Beach."

For the search teams, the problem was not finding bodies but identifying them. Many are so bloated it is impossible to tell their sex, never mind their nationality.

Throughout the region more than 3,500 foreigners were unaccounted for, among them at least 1,500 Swedes, 800 Norwegians, 214 Danes and 200 Finns.

Hundreds of people were killed in the Maldives, Myanmar and Malaysia. The arc of water struck as far away as Somalia and Kenya.

The region has seen huge killer waves before, including one when Krakatoa, off southern Sumatra, erupted in 1883 but Indian Ocean countries have no tsunami warning system.

(Remit: 3765 victims still unaccounted for, searching entry points L75, N89, Q94, S32, T91 Sector Asia).

6

'This is a wind up, right?' Joey said. He felt his stomach turn. If this were true, this was very bad. Very bad indeed. His mind was spinning like a reel unravelling cotton. 'Tell me this is a joke.'

'It's no joke, son,' Franklin said. His tone was sombre. 'There's a lot of folk out there who need picking up.'

'I can't believe that,' he said. 'I refuse to believe any of this.'

'I know you do, son.' He jerked his head toward the smoke outside. 'That's why you have to experience what's happening out there.'

Joey shook his head slowly. 'No,' he said. 'I don't.'

'That's fine, son. But sooner or later you'll have to face facts. You're dead. The people out there are dead. Death happens all the time. Sometimes it's peaceful, other times it's painful. Some folk have the time to prepare themselves for death because of a terminal illness. Their loved ones gather round and the transition to the after life is made a little easier with familiar faces. But sometimes the folk who are accident victims – victims of violent death – now they aren't so fortunate, son.'

He resisted the urge to ask why. He knew that Franklin J Merryhill was in preacher mode again. He let him rant, pretending not to listen.

Joey looked out the window at the billowing black funnel of smoke. There were dark figures silhouetted out there against a backdrop of dark and light.

'Death is the only event which we can predict with absolute confidence,' Franklin said, 'and yet it is the event about which the majority of human beings refuse to think at all until faced with the impending and personal issue.'

'Right,' Joey said, disturbed by the silhouetted figures massing a few hundred yards from the screen of smoke. They were too far away to see clearly. They reminded him of street corner gangs converging for something sinister.

'People face death in many different ways,' Franklin said, 'some bring to the adventure a feeling of self-pity, and are so busy with what they have to leave behind, what is about to end for them, and the letting go of all they have gathered in life, that the true result of the inevitable future fails to get their attention.'

'Right,' Joey muttered. The dark gang was expanding. Figures were coming swiftly from the out-lying woods. Some just seemed to impossibly appear from nowhere. This is weird shit, Joey thought.

'Others face it with courage,' Franklin went on, 'making the best of what may not be escaped, and look up into the face of death with a courageous shrug because there is nothing else they can do...

'Still others refuse altogether to consider the possibility; they hypnotize themselves into a condition where the thought of death is refused in their consciousness. They will not consider its possibility, so that when it comes, it catches them unawares; they are left helpless and unable to do more than simply die.'

'Right,' Joey said. 'Interesting.'

He had idly scanned the newspaper column next to the horrific tsunami story. At the bottom, he caught sight of his own name. His heart quickened. He read:

Treacherous Conditions Kills Five

Snow and ice are the cause of a crash in Dalton County that killed five people.

The accident happened at the intersection of route 28 and Lewfield Road in Georgetown. The car with all the victims inside tried to stop but could not, and slid right into an intersection where it was hit by a truck.

"They were travelling south on Lewfield Road and the road was slippery because of blowing, drifting snow and hard-packed ice. They were not able to stop for the intersection and entered route 28 in the path of a truck that was going westbound," said Dalton County Sheriff, George McVee.

Frank Moreton was at work when the accident occurred. "I was actually at my desk when I heard a loud crash, looked out the window and saw a truck pushing a car across that street into a ditch," said Moreton.

Moreton ran across the street and tried to help get 22-year old Louis Bell of Maine and four female friends out of the car. Emergency crews got there soon after and realized all were dead.

They had just left Bell's parent's house on Lewfield Road after a visit. A third car that couldn't avoid the crash scene was also involved, but no one in that car or the truck was hurt, and no one is being ticketed.

Sheriff McVee said Louis Bell and the women were students at a college in Maine. They were headed to New York City because they'd got tickets to see one of hip-hop-rock singer Joey Steffano's week-long sell-out shows at Madison Square Garden. They were then supposed to go to visit Bell's family in Maine.

(Remit: 2 road accident victims still unaccounted for. Keep searching entry point F934, Sector United States).

7

Joey recoiled from the article. It all came flooding back. Well, most of it. The flashing silver dollar, the overwhelming pain in his head, the fall and more pain.

Then the dark and numbness engulfed him. Then what next? He couldn't remember. A blank. Missing time, or was it missing consciousness? Whatever. The next memory was sitting onboard this prison on wheels, reading his *own* obituary.

'What is this? Another sick joke?'

'Do I look as if I'm laughing, son?' Franklin J Merryhill said. He folded the newspaper neatly in half and laid it down on the empty seat beside him. 'We've got a lot of work to do, son. First we'll round up as many as we can from the suicide bomb, then we'll help out with the tsunami disaster, and then it's on to see if we can find those fans of yours. There are a lot of lost souls out there.'

Joey nodded, distracted. He gazed at the gathering hoard of dark figures. They looked more like a crowd than a gang now. It was worrying. Were they the creatures Franklin had spoken about? Lost souls? Evil entities? Cut it out, Joey Steffano, he scolded. You're spooking yourself.

He jerked his eyes away from the scene. This was crazy. How many times would he tell himself that? And how many times would nothing change? No matter how hard he wished to wake up, or simply get up and walk through a magic door back into his old life, it just wasn't happening. He had to give himself a break before his mind snapped. He had to keep it light and loose. Franklin was right there, at least. He was in danger of losing his mind. Either the horror stories he'd read were true or not. Either he was dead, or he wasn't. For a dream, he thought, softening a little, this one has run a long time and is frighteningly vivid.

'What does that entry point and Sector stuff mean at the bottom of the stories?' Joey said, trying desperately not to over-react again.

'Exactly what it says, son. We're approaching entry point B73, Sector Middle East. Forty-two suicide bomb victims are still unaccounted for.'

The train was slowing.

Franklin raised two open palms and nodded toward the landscape outside. 'You coming, superstar?'

Joey's heart raced. A chance to get off maybe. Things were looking up. He felt light and loose. This was his chance. He couldn't believe the old guy was serious about letting him off. He touched the knife in his pocket; felt reassured that his blade was still there if things got a little out of hand. 'Where are we going, old man?'

'Entry point B73, Sector Middle East.' Franklin motioned to the blanket of acrid smoke which was a few hundred yards away. 'Just like you, there'll be a lot of folk who won't believe they're dead. Ninety-two poor souls is a big task. Of course, many of them have connected with their loved ones. So we've just got to round up the strays.'

'What do you mean – connect?'

'At the point of death, the victim's family who've already died gather to greet and comfort their loved ones.'

'If that's true, then why didn't my grandfather meet and greet me?'

'Because you don't believe you're dead, son. You're on the Journey's End train because of that simple fact.'

'So are you saying that the moment I *believe* I'm dead, my grandfather will appear out of thin air?'

'Something like that.'

'What happens next?'

'He'll help you settle in to your new life. Take you to your new home, a place he has already built for you.'

'Right,' Joey said. But he couldn't hide the sarcastic tone of his voice.

The train's brakes squealed like a wounded elephant.

'Some people are very lucky. They have family support at the point of entry, but many newly dead are not so lucky. Their minds are fogged. Loved ones can't break that fog. That's where the Journey's End team steps in. We round up as many of the lost as we can and in time most step outside the fog and see that the sun is shining, that they are still alive. There's no such thing as death, son. Did I tell you that?'

'Probably, a hundred times already, but I don't buy it.'

'I know.'

He looked out the window. 'Do your best out there, son. Just get as many of them onboard as quickly as you can.'

Joey bit on his lip. He was going to scoff at the old guy's crazy claims. No, not scoff, but crack up totally. He fought to keep the rising corners of his mouth from smiling. Ninety-two dead? Forty-two still out there, lost and confused? Get them onboard as quickly as you can? Do your best? What was this bullshit?

'Why the rush?' He decided to play along, to buy time. Keep it loose and light.

'It's not safe out there for too long.'

'Why is that? Is the bogey man lurking out there?' he laughed.

Joey looked out the window at the gathering crowd of

shadows, thickening now as though winter clouds.

'It's no joke, as you can see. It's a wilderness. It's a jungle of predators.'

'Right,' Joey said, nodding, struggling to hold back a smirk. Cut out the wise cracks, he told himself. I think this guy's a machine that got stuck in a loop or something. He keeps saying the same thing over and over.

'Discontented souls many of them, stalkers, the lost, the confused, nomads who refuse to believe the fact that they are dead. And of course the downright pig-headed.' He looked at Joey and smiled. 'No offence, son. But you ain't easy, now are you?'

Joey raised an eyebrow and returned the smile. Despite himself, despite his gut feeling not to trust him, he was starting to like the old guy, Franklin. You never knew whether he was joking or not. Joey thought that most of the time he was probably not. But this whole situation was so ludicrous that a little comedy made it more bearable.

He rubbed his chin. It felt as real as it ever did.

'Oh, and a couple of things you should know.'

'What are they?' said Joey, sounding really pissed off.

'Don't be a fool and try to make a break for it. It's a dangerous, confused place as I've said.'

'Right,' he said. 'I get the picture. I get the message, loud and clear.'

'Predators and stalkers roam that wilderness, looking for their next victim. Some work alone, but as you can see…' He paused for effect and nodded to the crowds of shadowy figures at the edge of the smoke. '…others are more organised. They hunt in packs – especially when so many dead are gathered all in one place.'

Joey's smile widened.

'It's no joke, superstar. Believe me.'

But Joey didn't believe him. The guy had gone on and on about how bad that wilderness was that Joey doubted him one hundred percent. It was an oversell, overkill, an over-the-top sale's pitch. He really had made up his mind to run for it. He would make a break for it the moment he got a clear chance.

'Right,' he said. 'Thanks for the advice, old guy.'

'No problem.'

His face hardened as he stood up. He looked formidable in his knee-length leather coat.

'And, son? My name's Franklin J Merryhill. I'm proud of that name, truly I am. You don't need to call me Mr Merryhill. Even though some folks might think that the most respectful thing for a stranger to call me. You can call me Franklin. Everyone around here does. But please don't call me old guy.' He patted his chest dramatically. 'It kind of hurts my heart, son. You understand that, don't you? Names are important to you, too, right?'

'Right,' Joey said, as they walked along the aisle to the open door. 'Didn't mean to cause offence, old, I mean, Franklin.'

8

A monotone announcement rang over the train's intercom: *B73, Sector Middle East. All rescue team members and associates follow your team leaders, please.*

Franklin nodded for Joey to follow him outside. Joey

walked just off the old guy's left shoulder, scanning the terrain. His eyes fixed on a distressing sight. He saw wafting plumes of acrid smoke and men, women and children, staggering out of it. Some of them were crying, others wringing hands and praying, but most simply milled about in a stunned silent shock. This was not what he'd expected.

Beyond, possibly a hundred yards away or less, he glimpsed the crowd of dark things lurking like a pack of silent wolves. He quickly followed Franklin like a dumb dog on his master's leash. This didn't feel good. In fact, Joey Steffano had a very bad feeling in the pit of his stomach.

He was unaware of the distant globe of light that was now the size of a small sun. It was racing toward him through the smoke.

Chapter Five

Angels

1

He was getting closer to the city, closer to pure water. Clean water. Water that would quench his deep thirst. He could almost smell it. Almost.

Was it a dream or a hallucination? Crack Boy wasn't sure; and he didn't care. It was bizarre and he was enjoying it in a banal kind of way. He was close, closer now than he'd ever been. There was nothing concrete in this feeling of surety; it was instinct. But it felt right, beyond hope. He was also waiting for the surprise. There was nearly always a surprise. Like the bits in horror movies that make you jump.

Joey and Eddie, and Jack's death, was a vague memory, a half-remembered incident from long ago. Time was so strange here, he thought. Time and memory. He was in a different place now, ever closer to the distant city sprawl. It was hot – uncomfortably so – and he'd been here before; several times, in fact. It was where the angels would come to tempt him. He knew that as surely as he knew his own name.

Let them come with their tricks and magic, he thought. I'll see right through their illusions. Their beauty and fine biblical words mean jack-shit to me. Propaganda merchants, that's all those angels are. They are as lost and confused with reality and its perception as I am. No, their confusion is greater. They actually believe all that shite they espouse.

But Crack Boy believed Life was bigger than any intellectual belief system. Life and Death. Yes, the big issues. Hadn't someone written a book about a Tree of Life and Death, about psychic shamutants living in sewers under a corrupt city, and about insectiant suicide bombing Pardoners?

Yes.

Maybe.

No.

He couldn't recall. He didn't read many books.

2

Clouds evaporated under the ferocity of the sun. It was so hot that any kind of movement was like stepping into a blast furnace in the blacksmith's forge at the end of the street where he lived when he was a kid. Basking, within an island of cypress trees in the middle of the creek's slow-moving current, was a ten-foot alligator. It lay motionless in the oppressive heat. Its glassy eyes mirrored the glare of the hot sky.

Crack Boy rolled his aching shoulders, tried but failed to shake off his tremors. The kick-back of crashing down from a Charlie-rope cocktail was the shivers and shakes. But there were more side-effects, he knew. Things were going to get a hell of a lot worse before they got better. There was only one thing that would make him feel better right now: more Charlie, more white.

Shake, rattle, and roll.

Sweat dripped from his nose. His clothes were saturated with it. His throat was as dry as a desert fire. He felt extremely fatigued. His eyes kept popping closed, snapping open like a bay alligator's jaw. He felt starved of oxygen, as if sitting in a vacuum heated by a wood burner.

Cicadas were too lethargic to make their grating music, although one assiduous insect sporadically troubled the drowsy atmosphere with a try that was really not worth the bother. A water moccasin lay unmoving on the bank, intimidating like a school bully. Fish lingered well below the surface of the water and its dense duckweed carpet. They quivered in the muddy depths, gills throbbing.

The swamp was an avian menagerie, but today every bird was snoozing in its nest, with the exclusion of a single crow. He was perched at the top of a tree that had been struck by lightning. The elements had bleached and picked clean its branches, leaving them stripped and white as bones.

Something zig-zagged beneath the water. Its motion created a ripple on the surface. Small but noticeable in the oppressive stillness. A dark long shadow undulated beneath the water, indistinct and ominous. It was heading toward Crack Boy's dangling toes. Higher it rose from the depths. Faster now. Up, up, up to shatter the surface with a mighty splash and blaze of penetrating white light.

Snap!

Smash!

*

3

Crack Boy snapped open his eyes from a confused vision which consisted of a single image: that of an angel he'd once smashed as a child with a brick. The angel back then had been a fifteen foot tall stained-glass church window. It had shattered into countless tiny shards of multi-coloured glass, raining down on the vicar and his Sunday morning parishioners. He'd been called Joseph White back then, and he was mid-way through his eighth year of life.

This angel, however, was close to seven foot tall, a woman of stunning beauty. A radiant white blue light shone from her skin like sunlight penetrating fine silk. She hovered a few feet above the swamp, water sizzling like fat in a pan from her naked body.

He thought wildly that a brick would do her no harm whatsoever. He was probably right, but he simply backed away deeper into the nearest swamp. It was wet and warm and crawling with creatures, but it was the least of his worries. Her light was too much, too bright.

'Leave me alone,' he said. He was shielding his eyes with his arm. It was a familiar plea, one which he'd rallied many times here in this dark world; for he knew why she was here, and what she aimed to do.

'Do not be afraid,' she said softly. 'I am neither a dream nor a nightmare. I have come to help you. Will you take the first step on the road to self-help, on the road back to the light, back to love?'

'Go talk your sanctimonious words to someone who gives a fuck,' Crack Boy snarled. 'Leave me alone. Leave me to my nightmare.'

'I can't. You know that.'

'I know that you are really pissing me off,' he said. 'Now back off…please. I want to be left alone.'

Pococin pine cones crackled in the heat. Some dropped, brittle things, shattering like glass. Trunks swayed and moaned and spat bark chips.

'No, I cannot do that.' She opened a large red leather-bound book. 'I must read and you must listen.'

'No!' he screamed, and he slipped a pistol out of its holster. 'I'll shoot you, you meddling bitch. Back off! I mean it. I'll shoot!'

The angel read.

To Crack Boy, it was like a pig reading him the right to remain silent. Her book and its words assaulted his intelligence, insulted his right to bask in the darkness of the dark world. She was no better than a soap box cleric; no worse than a cable channel preacher. But she was stunningly beautiful, radiantly glamorous.

Hallelujah and amen.

She heard his thoughts but she read on anyway.

'Some of the inhabitants had lived here, or hereabouts, year after year – as time is reckoned upon earth. They themselves had no sense of time, and their existence had been one everlasting continuity of darkness through no one's fault but their own. Many had been the good souls who had penetrated into these Stygian realms to try to affect a rescue out of the darkness. Some had been successful; others had not. Success depends not so much upon the rescuer as upon the rescued. If the latter shows no glimmer of light in his mind, no longing to take a step forward on the spiritual road, then nothing, literally nothing, can be done. The compulsion *must* come from within the fallen soul himself. And how low some of them had plummeted!'

'Please,' Crack Boy said. 'Just back off.'

The Smith and Wesson trembled in his hand. He knew that the trigger was stiff, even after so many rounds. It took a full eight pounds of pull to fire it. He aimed where he guessed the angel's heart might be. He was going to do it.

She carried on regardless. Her words hit him like missiles, making him wince.

'Never must it be thought that those who, in the earth's judgment, had failed spiritually, are fallen low. Many such souls have not failed at all, but are, in point of fact, worthy souls whose fine reward awaits them here. But on the other hand, there are those whose earthly lives have been spiritually hideous though outwardly sublime; whose religious profession nominated by a arch-bishop's collar, has been taken for granted as being tantamount with spirituality of soul. Such people have been mocking God throughout their sanctimonious lives on earth where they lived with a hollow display of holiness and goodness. Here they stand revealed for what they are. But the God they have ridiculed for so long does not punish.'

'I know,' he said lamely. 'We punish ourselves. You have told me this too many times, angel. It means very little to me. I understand it, but really I don't give a damn. Leave me alone!'

'*They punish themselves.*'

He fired the pistol at the angel's heart.

Three times in quick succession.

Bang! Bang! Bang!

She carried on reading. Her words were like bullets themselves.

'The people living within these hovels in this dark world that we were passing were not necessarily those who upon earth had committed some crime in the eyes of the earth people. There were many people who, without doing any harm, *had never, never done any good to a single mortal upon earth.* People who had lived entirely unto themselves, without a thought for others. Such souls constantly harped upon the theme that they had done no *harm* to anyone. But they had harmed themselves.'

'I'm going to fucking well harm you,' Crack Boy yelled, and he fired half a dozen times at the blinding light. 'Back off! Shut up!'

'As the higher spheres had created all the beauties of those realms, so had the denizens of those lower spheres built up the appalling conditions of their spirit life. There was no light in the lowest realms; no warmth, no vegetation, no beauty. But there is hope – hope that every soul there will progress. It is in the power of each soul to do so, and nothing stands in his way but himself. It may take him countless thousands of years to raise himself one inch spiritually, but it is an inch in the right direction.'

'I'll not give an inch. Take this!'

Crack Boy fired off another volley of shots into the angel.

Her beautiful naked body was riddled with bullet holes. Golden rays flooded through them like nightclub up-lighters. All she needs to do next, Crack Boy thought, is to spin like a freakin' strobe and sing 'J-J-J-Jive talking; telling me lies!'

She read on.

He winced.

'The thought inevitably came into my mind of the doctrine of eternal damnation, so beloved by orthodox religion, and of the everlasting fires of so-called hell. If this place we were now could be called hell – and no doubt it would be by theologians – then there was certainly no evidence of fire or heat of any kind.'

'You are joking!' Crack Boy yelled, sweat dripping from his nose. 'This is the hottest place I know!'

'On the divergent, there was nothing but a cold, dank atmosphere. Spirituality means warmth in the spirit world; lack of spirituality means coldness. The whole fantastic principle of hell-fire – a fire which burns but never consumes – is one of the most outrageously obtuse and ignorant doctrines that has ever been invented by equally obtuse and ignorant churchmen. Who actually invented it no one knows, but it is still rigorously upheld as a doctrine by the church. Even the smallest acquaintance with spirit life instantly reveals the utter impossibility of it, because it is against the very laws of spirit existence. This concerns its literal side. What of the shocking blasphemy that it involves?

'When you were on earth we were asked to believe that God, the Father of the Universe, punishes, *actually punishes* people by condemning them to burn in the flames of hell for all eternity. Could there ever be any grosser travesty of the God that orthodoxy professes to worship? The churches – of whatever denomination –

have built up a monstrous conception of the Eternal Father of Heaven. They have made of Him, on the one hand, a mountain of corruption by shallow lip service, by spending large sums of money to erect churches and chapels to His 'glory', by pretending a grovelling contrition for having 'offended Him', by professing to fear Him – *fear* Him who is all love! And on the other hand, we have the picture of a God who, without the slightest compunction, casts poor human souls into an eternity of the worst of all sufferings – burning by fires that are unquenchable.'

His ears were burning, his mind whirling with words.

'Shut the fuck up!'

Bang! Bang! Bang!

'You were taught persuasively to beg for God's mercy. The church's God is a being of extraordinary moods. He must be continually appeased. It is by no means certain that, having begged for mercy, we shall get it. He must be feared – because He can bring down His vengeance upon us at any moment; we do not know when He will strike. He is vengeful and unforgiving. He has commanded such trivialities as are embodied in church doctrines and dogmas that at once expose not a great mind, but a small one. He has made the doorway to 'salvation' so slender that few souls will ever be able to pass through it. He has built up on the earth-plane a vast organization known as 'the Church', which shall be the sole reservoir of spiritual truth – an organization that knows practically *nothing* of the state of life in the world of spirit, yet *dares* to lay down the law to incarnate souls, and *dares* to say what is in the mind of the Great Father of the Universe, and *dares* to discredit His Name by assigning to Him characteristics that *He could not possibly possess.* What do such juvenile, petty minds know of the Great and Almighty Father of Love? Mark that! – *God* of *Love.* Then think again of all the horrors I have catalogued. And think once more. Contemplate this: a heaven of all that is beautiful, a heaven of more beauty than the mind of man incarnate can comprehend; a heaven, of which one tiny fragment I have tried to describe to you, where all is peace and goodwill and love among fellow mortals. All these things are built up by the inhabitants of these realms, and are upheld by the Father of Heaven in His love for *all* mankind.'

'No!'

'Yes, Joseph White. Yes. Hold out your hand. Take the first step. Make the first move. Use your own free will. Come with me to a place of love and light and-'

'No!'

Another angel appeared next to the one talking. Then another and another. Their combined light was overwhelming. Their love beleaguered him. Another one spoke now.

'What of the lower realms – the dark world we are now visiting?'

It sounded like a child's questioning voice.

'Why are you letting a child see me?' Crack Boy said, sounding ashamed and offended. 'No child should ever come here to this dark world.'

'It is the very fact that we are visiting them that has led me to speak in this fashion,' spoke the first angel, speaking not to Crack Boy but to the child, 'because

118

standing in this darkness I am fully conscious of one great reality of eternal life, and that is that the high spheres of heaven are within the reach of every mortal soul that is, or is yet to be, born upon earth. The potentialities of development are unlimited, and they are the right of every soul. God censures no one.'

'Man condemns himself,' said another voice, a man's smooth low tones, 'but he does not condemn himself eternally; it rests with himself as to when he shall move forward spiritually.'

'Yes,' said the first angel. 'Every spirit abhors the dark worlds for the unhappiness that is there, and for no other reason. And for that reason great organizations exist to help every single soul who is living in them to rise out of them into the light. And that work will continue through countless ages until every soul is brought out from these hideous places, and at last all is as the Creator of the Universe intended it to be.'

'Leave me be,' Crack Boy sobbed. He was shaking now, hugging his knees, as the water soaked him. He rocked to and fro. The gun swung loosely on his index finger by its trigger. He would not shoot it now. 'Take the child away.'

He fell over, rolled into the water, and buried his face in its wetness. This was the way to end it. This was the way to end the nightmare. But please take the child away.

He blew bubbles into the water for the last time.

But, no – this was no nightmare. It was a fine dream. It was fine because *he* was the one drowning, and that meant he was not Crack Boy at all but Joey. This thought was some comfort because it would be better to die as

Joey in this pool of water than to live as himself, a man who had lost control and filled his body full of drugs, and selfishness and greed.

Yes, that's fine, I'll drown, he thought, listening to the lap of the swamp, hearing the final flurry of bubbles leave his lips. *Let me drown, Angels. Let me be no more.*

Yet there was another sound, the sound of something large entering the water. It could have been one of a handful of predators that inhabited the swamps. He could feel the undercurrent of that something winding its way toward him. He waited for the crunch of his bones that would hopefully end it.

4

'Help me, please.'

Crack Boy's left ear was out of the water, even though his face was submerged. His head felt as if it was about to implode. His lungs felt the same – searing heat that made him desperate to gulp in oxygen that would be water suffocating instead. A screaming pain assaulted his brain, like the very worst migraine imaginable.

'Help, me. I'm scared. Where am I?'

Crack Boy whipped his head out of the water, gasping for breath, spluttering. He coughed and gagged violently as he dragged himself out of the swamp on his hands and knees, which was rolling now with the force of the predator heading in his direction.

He stood up on soaking shaky legs, backed away from the danger onto solid ground and squinted into the thick tangle of trees. He was bent double, hands planted firmly on his knees, surveying the forest.

The angels had gone.

Less than fifteen yards away, he saw her and was stunned. He breathed in burning, hot air in deep, indulgent gulps.

A young woman crouched like a cornered animal. She was in the middle of an indistinct trail on a ribbon of dry land running through a dense swamp. The weak light from a dark, overcast sky barely breached the bald cypress forest as she wrapped her arms around herself and quivered, trying to catch her breath. She had been running, almost to exhaustion. But from whom or what?

Crack Boy felt a hot wave of compassion for her, an inexplicable desire to protect her. Why? She wasn't crew. She was a woman, and women were trouble. That attitude had been drummed into him since he was eleven. He'd not questioned its validity, he'd found nothing to disprove the axiom. It was just another blind belief that made up much of his psyche. If nothing else, he was extreme in many of his beliefs.

She wore nothing to guard her from the elements but a ragged, coarse, homespun dress and an ill-fitting pair of leather moccasins that had worn blisters on her heels.

Despite her clothing, Crack Boy was transfixed by her stunning beauty. Was she another angel?

5

Where am I?

She gazed around, her eyes pulsing, her head dizzy with the lack of breath. What is this place?

She knew who she was and why she was here. Her name was Javanah. She turned her head and smiled slyly so that Crack Boy could not see her twisted lips.

Around her, like a discarded shell, were the remnants of the globe of light she had travelled in. It seeped into the undergrowth like water, gurgling. So far, so deep. Gone.

The primordial path was nearly eradicated by lichen and fern that grew over deep drifts of dried twigs and leaves. Here and there it was strewn with larger, decomposing, fallen limbs of trees. The copious odour of decay hung in the air, pushing down on her, bracing her trepidation.

Her breathing was fast and hard. It had been such a long arduous journey. She looked sideways through her tousled raven hair, pushed it back, her fingers marbled with blood. Her hands trembled. Terror born of being lost was heightened by the knowledge that night was going to fall before she found her way out of the swamp. But she took comfort, small though it was, from the fact that she knew her name and why she was here. The first she saw would be the One. The first she saw was always the One. Javanah was nothing if not certain about her purpose.

Not only did the encroaching darkness frighten her, but so did the deep, silent waters along both sides of the trail. It was alien here, utterly, totally. Realizing she would soon be surrounded by night and water both, a strangled cry escaped her. She hated the dark, bathed only in red light.

Behind her, from somewhere deep amid the cypress trees, wrapped in rust-coloured bark, she heard a splash. Some unseen creature dropped into the watery ooze.

She rose, spun around and scanned the surface of the swamp. Frogs and fish, venomous copperheads and turtles big as frying pans thrived beneath the lacy emerald carpet of duckweed that floated upon the water. As she knelt there, wondering whether she should continue in the same direction or turn back, she watched a small knot of fur skim over the surface of the water toward her.

This was not the One. The One would be detectable by the stench of his soul. She sniffed the air like a hound. The One was close.

A soaking wet muskrat lost its grace as soon as it made land and lumbered up the bank in her direction. Almost amused and yet wary, the young woman scrambled back a few inches. The creature froze and stared back with dark, beady eyes before it turned tail, hit the water and disappeared.

Forcing herself to her feet, Javanah kept her eyes trained on the narrow footpath, gingerly stepping through piles of damp, decayed leaves. Again she paused, lifted her head, listened for the sound of a human voice, the pounding footsteps which meant someone was in pursuit of her along the trail.

When all she heard was the distant knock of a woodpecker, she let go a sigh of relief. Determined to keep moving, she trudged on, ever vigilant, hoping that the edge of the swamp lay just ahead.

Suddenly, the sharp, shrill scream of a bobcat set her heart hammering. With a fist pressed against her lips, she compressed her eyes closed and froze, afraid to move, afraid to even breathe.

Adrenalin pumped and she fought the urge to take

flight. It was dangerous here, but what she possessed was far worse. She took little comfort from the fact.

All was alien. She hated being away from her domain of red light.

The cat shrieked again, and the cry echoed across the haunting silence of the swamp until it seemed to rouse the very air around her.

She glanced up at dishwater navy blue scraps of weak twilight nearly eliminated by the cypress trees that grew so close together in some places that not even a small child could pass between them. There was a dark shadowy figure standing on the far bank. It looked almost human, almost. But it seemed too insubstantial, like the pale shadow of a ghost.

It waved at her.

She sniffed the air again.

An alien thing in an alien environment.

It was the One.

She smirked a little now that her prey was in clear sight.

6

Crack Boy waved at her.

She looked scared stiff. He felt even more compassion toward her, which was so unlike him. She got up at the sound of the wild cat and ran – in the opposite direction.

'Wait!' Crack Boy called out. 'I won't harm you.'

She glimpsed over her shoulder, eyes wide with fear. She kept running. She kept running as fast as her weak legs would carry her.

7

The sound of the shadowy ghost-human calling out to her and the thought that a wild cat might be looming somewhere above her in the tangled limbs, crouched and ready to pounce, sent her running down the narrow, winding trail like a hundred metre sprinter.

'Come on, One,' she whispered to herself. 'Take the bait. Follow me.'

She had not gone more than fifty strides when the toe of her shoe wedged beneath an exposed tree root. Catapulted forward, she began to fall and wailed out.

Loud.

Mock anguish.

Another hideous cry of pain.

As the forest floor rushed up to meet her, she put out her hands to break her fall. A shock of pain blasted through her wrist an instant before her head hit a log. She heard her toes snap...

And then her world went dark.

8

As he began to run after the woman, he became aware of something both embarrassing and alarming. Pleasantly warm water had drenched his Nike trainers and had scurried up his legs to his crotch. Damn, he thought. Damn, damn, damn!

He looked down at the damp patch, and what ripped him out of the vision wasn't his luke warm testicles, which made him feel like he'd pissed himself. No. It wasn't the young woman running ahead of him but the significance of his Smith and Wesson semi-automatic pistols, and even more crucial, his bullets. Wet guns were easy to dismantle, to dab dry, lubricate, dab dry again, lubricate once more, and put back together. Wet shells were like wet matches – they probably wouldn't work again.

All I need is one bullet. One shot will do it.

He carried on running, gaining on her slightly. Dead leaves crunched beneath his soggy trainers.

If he was going to kill himself, he couldn't have chosen a worse day for it. He was feeling so low and useless after the angel's rant, so desperate for a fix of something, anything to get him through, that the obvious hadn't registered until now.

Now he doubted that his guns would work. How stupid!

You are stupid and useless, Sonny Joe.

He ignored the voice. He'd killed his step-father, hadn't he? But the voice was right. He was stupid.

You're so stupid. Just listen to your crazy talk. Crack Boy has finally cracked up.

Not funny.

He laughed anyway, hollow and coarse, and his laughter rebounded off the hard brittle bark of cypress trees and laughed back at him. Like a kookaburra.

'I'm already dead,' he said numbly. 'So why don't I feel dead? Why do I feel so alive?'

The atmosphere was as thick and hot as pan-fried syrup. It sucked the energy right out of every living thing. He wished it would suck it out of him and have done with it. Still, even with the cloying heat, he ran harder along a barely recognisable track. This was not the Yellow Brick Road.

His wet gun problem gave way to the young woman, screaming. He saw her fall ahead of him, and now sprinted as fast as he could.

The bob-cat has taken her down, he thought, fear rising up inside his gut. I'm gonna face a wild cat with a gun that doesn't fire.

But as he approached the motionless body, another much larger problem loomed.

Chapter Six

The Wilderness

1

Joey watched Franklin enter the smoke. He was speaking to people in their own language and they were talking back. Half a dozen shell-shocked individuals followed him out. He motioned them on towards the open train doors. They were coughing and spluttering and many of them were bleeding from face and body wounds.

The dark pack of creatures began to fan out, moving steadily toward him.

'Don't just stand there, son. Either run away or help us,' he said as he hurried by Joey and vanished into more smoke. 'That's what you do best, isn't it? Running away?'

Joey opened his mouth to reply, but he shut it again. Franklin had appeared like a black ghost, holding a limp young girl in his arms.

'Here, take her,' he said, carefully placing the child into Joey's arms. 'Put her down on the seats. Hurry. I'll need you to help lift out the next guy. He must weigh over two hundred pounds.'

The pack was howling now. They sped across the open countryside toward them.

Joey turned, speechless, and jogged across the muddy ground. It was less then twenty yards to the train. He was met at the threshold by Annie. She took the child from him, nodded her acknowledgement of his heroic deed, and hurried inside. He felt like a complete fraud. He felt the sides of his face burn red with embarrassment and shame.

Joey turned quickly, immersed in the trauma now. More injured people were staggering out of the smoke. He told them to get on the train as fast as they could, pointed and motioned toward the open doors. He guessed the language they replied with was Arabic, but he wasn't sure. Geography and linguistics were not something he'd studied too much. They seemed to get the message though, and they helped one another across the slippery mud to the train.

Ellen and Harry slipped into the smoke fifteen yards away. They were carrying a stretcher, Ellen leading the way. Moments later they came out with a badly bleeding young woman onboard. They jogged toward the front carriages, which Joey could see now. There must have been another twenty carriages from the front to the ripped-in-half rear. At least five of them, closest to the engine, had 'Medical Emergency Carriage' written on the outside in large blue letters.

He covered his nose and mouth with the crook of his arm as he entered the smoke. He sidled like a crab, his free hand outstretched against anything that he might encounter.

Now's your chance, he thought. Take it. You don't believe the old guy's bullshit, do you?

He didn't, but through squinted, watering eyes he saw the smoke clear. Ahead he saw Franklin, who put a thumb up. Ellen and Harry were helping Franklin to roll the two hundred pound man onto the stretcher. Joey wasn't needed there.

To his left, Joey counted. Five cars had erupted in flames and a dozen or so passenger minibuses had been destroyed. Medical workers were already amongst the living injured, struggling to treat people suffering from severe lacerations and burns. Ambulance sirens wailed and several policemen were cordoning off the area, driving away onlookers.

The crowded bus station was littered with shrapnel, broken glass, and bodies; injured, sobbing, screaming people. Rising out of the motionless bodies of the dead were replicas. They were clearly alive. These were not misty ghosts at all. They looked real and solid. Many were trying to comfort the living injured. But those still alive, strewn and bleeding on the road near the crater where the bomb had exploded, couldn't see the replica bodies of the dead who attempted to attend to their needs. It was a bizarre sight, Joey thought.

As Franklin had said back on the train, many of the victims were being greeted by dead family members. They were shedding tears of joy and relief. People hugged and kissed, amazed by their reunions. Moments later they hurried down tunnels of light that were opening up all over the place like worm holes.

The light engulfed them. They ran arm in arm along the tunnels. There were giggling, raised voices of ecstasy.

The worm holes closed.

Joey had no time to consider what he'd seen. He heard the howling pack beyond the smoke baying now. They were very close.

He scanned the scene of carnage before him.

'This way!' he yelled, beckoning to a group of teenagers who were stunned to discover that they were out of their bodies. 'Hurry.'

Even though they spoke in Arabic, Joey understood every word somehow.

'Do you think we are going with you, American filth?' the tallest boy said.

The smallest boy, possibly eight or nine years old, spat in Joey's direction.

'You are to blame for this,' said the tallest. 'Go fuck yourself, American pig.'

'It's a suicide bomber, one of your own people,' Joey said, unable to recall many of the details from the newspaper report Franklin had shown him.

'Fuck you, arsehole.'

The gang of seven boys strode toward Joey. The oldest was possibly thirteen, a good deal shorter than Joey. The others weren't much older than ten or eleven. He was a man; they were kids. He held out his hands in a 'back-off' gesture.

But they kept coming.

Gang warfare, he thought, without any irony in his mind.

He backed off three steps, then decided to stand his ground. He knew the rules of the street, and he guessed they did, too. Iraq or America? He thought that on the street all was the same. The gun and the knife ruled. He slipped his hand into his pocket, his heart really pounded hard now. He felt the crazy kick of adrenaline punch into his bloodstream. Fight or flight.

They kept coming, swearing and cursing him.

Joey Steffano, boss of The Breakers, stood his ground. This is stupid, he thought. 'I'm here to help you, guys. Not fight.'

They ran at him, yelling.

He took out his knife and the six inch blade flashed from the handle. He raised it before him, waving it in a slow arc so that they could clearly see it.

They kept coming, slower now, but still they weren't backing off, knife or not.

They're crazy, Joey thought. Don't they realise that they're already dead?

'You're dead, for fuck sake. Can't you see that?' Joey shouted.

What did I say?

Joey would have recoiled if he'd had time. He couldn't believe he'd said that. Did he really believe it? If so, according to the doctrine of Franklin J Merryhill, one of those light-filled worm holes should open up and his dead grandfather – James White – should be making an appearance at any moment.

The boys were circling Joey – just far enough away from his blade, but much too close for comfort. Joey was swivelling on one motionless foot, eyes everywhere, guarding his back, flashing the blade at anyone who got close.

If they are dead, then so are you, son. Joey heard Franklin's velvet voice in his head. The horrific realization hit him hard. And if they are dead, and you are dead, then fighting them is a waste of time. Unless the dead can kill the dead?

As the first boy, the leader, charged toward him with his fists flailing, Joey side-stepped him, pushing him hard between his shoulder blades with his open hand. The kid skidded across the circle, and hit the ground with a smack. Dust puffed up around him.

The rest of his gang backed off, dragging him away a few yards, clambering around their leader, helping him to his feet.

He did *not* feel dead, Joey thought, aghast. He was solid. Real. And I don't see James White and his halo of gold light?

'I could have cut you bad, you stupid sonnafa bitch,' Joey screamed, pumped up. 'Now back off!'

The kid got up and screamed at Joey, launching himself at him again.

Joey withdrew the blade seconds before the kid lunged at him with a miss-timed right hook. He could have cut the kid again, but this was stupid. Instead, he hooked him with a left on the point of his chin.

The kid hit the dusty ground with a thump.

He was unconscious.

Joey stepped over the kid, straddled him in a sign of superiority.

He held the bladeless knife in his hand. He scanned the rest of the quieter gang members. They were looking sheepish now, not sure what to do next.

Joey looked across at Franklin as he emerged from the smoke. 'You finished here, son?' he said.

Joey nodded. He walked toward Franklin, away from the gang to give them some space. He stopped at the edge of the smoke that bordered two worlds.

'You coming? Or staying?' he said to them, and he winced slightly because he sounded like Franklin now.

They all looked up simultaneously, and Joey saw himself in their eyes before he became the boss of The Breakers. Fear of failure, dread of being left out. The peer pressure was enormous.

'Bring him with you,' Joey said, pointing at the motionless kid on the ground. He was already regretting the invitation. He knew that the crazy kid was trouble. He'd known many kids like him. They always acted before they thought things through. They were the first to die in a street battle. Fearless, crazy, and stupid.

He motioned to the carnage all around. 'There's nothing for you here now.'

Sheepishly, the children picked up their unconscious leader between them and followed Joey Steffano into the smoke.

2

Joey stepped out of the smoke and stopped abruptly. A half circle of dark figures were fanned out around him, Franklin, Ellen, Harry, and the boys. There must have been a hundred or more and they stood between the smoke and the safety of the train.

Joey saw that the train doors had been closed and a thin zig-zag pulse of what looked like blue electricity crackled up and down the train's shell. Was it protection, a kind of force-field? Or had the creatures used it to imprison the people onboard? Whatever the answer, it was obvious he had lingered too long in the Wilderness.

'Don't run, whatever else you do – do not run,' Franklin said with a low, hard edge to his voice.

'Why not?' Joey whispered back hoarsely.

'These folk aren't exactly friends, son. You understand me?'

'Right.' Joey said. 'I kinda got that impression myself.'

'You foolin' with me, son?'

Joey smirked. Another time, another place he would have cracked a laugh, but the dark figures were edging closer, shrinking the circle.

'If we don't run, then what do we do? Fight?'

'In a way, son.' Franklin moved boldly three steps toward the figures. 'But it's not the kind of street fighting you know.'

'Right,' Joey said. 'What kind is it then?'

'Love,' he said. 'It has the power to heal and clean.'

'Right,' Joey said. 'I wondered what you had hidden inside your coat. You're gonna arm yourself with a bottle of Domestos, right?'

'You're funny, son.' Franklin opened his leather coat wide, like wings. 'Might be best if you shield your eyes.'

3

Joey took out his flick knife and pressed the button which released the shimmering blade. He was going to quip again about the Power of Love and Peace, and drop in a smart-arse comment about – *just look where that misplaced ideology got John Lennon* – when he was blinded by the light.

He staggered sideways to Franklin's left. He tried to

peek through fingers that covered his face. It was like looking up at a tidal wave of light – white and overwhelming. It was harsher than sunlight, but strangely it did not burn.

He stepped back a few paces, so that he was behind Franklin now. The old guy still had his coat held open like a taut sail in a stiff breeze. From it the light poured like a fluxing liquid-solid force. Bizarrely it seemed solid *and* liquid at the same time. A paradoxical insight, Joey knew, but it would stay with him for a long time.

The light rose like a tsunami, its crest fully fifty feet high. The waves of light rolled over one another. The darkness in its path seemed to be sucked like black sludge down a gigantic plughole.

The dark figures screamed now, charging like a baying pack of wolves towards them.

'Hold your ground,' Franklin said from within the light, which completely swamped him. 'Do not run. Stand firm!'

The screaming entities deafened Joey. He covered his ears, dropping his blade. They tightened the circle like a strangler's hands around a soft throat.

'Do not run!'

Through squinting eyes Joey saw the fastest, closest creatures bowled over. They got to within twenty feet of Franklin and then…wham!

The earth opened.

A whirlpool of light erupted where the entities fell, dragging them into the vortex. Screaming, spitting.

The hole closed.

They were gone.

The light from Franklin's coat stretched behind him, engulfed them all. More holes opened and more entities vanished within them.

One entity managed to grab hold of a thick root protruding from the earth where a vortex was sucking him down. He cried for mercy, tears staining his rotten, fleshless face.

Joey felt something from the entity's plea. Something tangible touched him, a raw finger of emotion.

Something.

The entity cried out again and Joey was touched by a deeper emotion – forgiveness.

In that moment of release, the vortex dragged the entity down, closed the earth like a door slammed in his face. A small depression was all that remained in the earth.

Stark.

Arcane.

There was something more humane entangling its tendril around Joey. Another vortex opened beside him. Another entity was clinging to a root, fighting the sucking black hole.

Joey stared in disbelief. It was the same dark creature that had separated from him on the train and leapt into the void. But worse – that entity was a mirror image.

Joey shook his head.

'No!' he screamed.

Joey's legs gave way.

Yes. It was him. His dark double.

Chapter Seven

Duality

1

Crack Boy was running as fast as he could.

Ahead of him was a blur of cypress branches and undergrowth. He saw the young woman laying face-down and motionless in the dirt and leaves. Her foot was tangled in the root. From the angle of her twisted leg, it looked like a bad break. She had both arms sprawled out in front of her, which was good. She had managed to break some of the fall.

But obviously not enough.

Was she unconscious?

Crack Boy tried to stop in time, but couldn't. He skidded sideways through the leaves. He flailed his arms out to slow his motion. But it was no use. Too little, too late.

He slipped into the gaping black hole, which opened just inches from the young woman's body. Dust and leaves flew up into his eyes. He coughed and spluttered, lungs filled with debris.

He yelled.

He clawed.

He reached out, grappling for a handhold, anything to grip. But he clenched handfuls of leaves and dry, sandy soil. His legs felt as if they had been dipped in an almost frozen plunge pool. A swirling vortex of light and dark whirled beneath him like cream stirred into black coffee.

'What the hell is this?' he screamed.

No-one answered.

He'd never experienced this scenario before. Surely this wasn't the doing of the angels? They wouldn't stoop so low, would they?

Somehow, he grasped the motionless woman's sleeve. It tore, he slipped, hand over hand, re-arranging his hold. The dark hole was trying to suck him down.

A spider in a giant plughole.

His weight ripped her arm like a child dislocating a plastic doll's arm from its socket. She jerked, but remained unconscious.

He grabbed her forearm with his left hand, and started to haul himself up. His weight shifted her weight again.

She lurched, pulled closer to the hole. Something else snapped on her body, but Crack Boy tried not to think about what that might have been. He thought only of survival. It had always been this way.

The vortex pulled harder, ripping his trousers down. They were dangling around his trainers, hooked. His genitals were exposed and shrivelled. His guns flapped like impotent things in their leather holsters around his waist. His jacket fluttered like a khaki flag of surrender.

He grappled, slipped, clung now to her limp hand. Her skin was so soft.

The vortex had frozen all feeling below his waist. The whipping winds numbed his chest now. The strength in his arms waned. He coughed, gagged for breath as the freezing wind choked him.

Let go, a cold calculating voice said in his head. It was Joey Steffano's voice. Jumped up little prick.

Let go now!

No, it wasn't Joey, it was steady Eddie Steffano.

Slippage.

Crack Boy heaved himself up in a last desperate attempt. He somehow managed to let go of the woman's ruined arm. His fingertips wrapped around the root next to her broken leg.

That's when she sat bolt upright, glaring insanely. 'Let go now!' she roared, spittle flying in thick flecks from her lips. 'Let go and accept your fate, you little arsehole!'

Crack Boy screamed.

Javanah punched him as hard as she could between the eyes.

It felt like a hammer blow.

Chapter Eight

Journey's End

1

Joey was standing next to Franklin, transfixed by the light spreading from his coat. It seemed to speak to him, not in words but in something beyond his comprehension.

Am I tripping? he thought.

The entity clinging to the root, sucked into the mouth of the vortex, cried out for mercy.

The light sighed as gently as a lapping ocean in answer to its plea. Within that concourse of light (which expanded its radius one hundred yards as though a wide-beamed searchlight), there were smaller golden specks of light. They danced and zigzagged in their billions. They were barely visible.

Joey glimpsed one, a tiny pin-prick, or so it seemed, until he was sucked toward the thing. That something was more than a plea. That something was a living thought, a breathing emotion. In an instant, the miniscule particle expanded – or maybe he shrank, he wasn't sure – and he saw a world within it.

This world was vast and blue and green and vibrant. There were scudding great clouds and verdant mountains and deep sparkling oceans. He drifted across winding rivers and forked tributaries.

'What is this?' he said, but his voice was flat and

echoless, as if spoken in his head.

No-one answered.

Volcanoes erupted columns of choking smoke and debris, and molten lava flowed like melting treacle down smouldering mountainsides.

Further and deeper. Vast tropical rainforests were cut down in swathes by large yellow machines. Islands laden with palm trees flickered before his eyes, only to be replaced with larger land masses – continents and sprawling cities and skyscrapers and cardboard hovels edged around the city limits, and now vast wastes of orange desert with immaculate pyramids pointing toward the darkness of space.

He gazed up, caught like a fly in an invisible web which had been spun everywhere into the blackness, its imperceptible gossamer wires linking one star to another star in an infinite labyrinth of star webs.

He was spinning as if trapped in slow-motion, like an astronaut cut loose in deep, cold soundless space. Smudges of galaxies and nebulae and merging universes trickled before his eyes, watery and translucent and evaporating.

'What is this?'

No-one answered. Not even an echo of his pointless question.

He threw up, dizzy and nauseated. His yellow vomit floated away as slowly as he did, away from that speck of the planet. How could something so small be so large? Micro-chip technology wasn't even a foetus by comparison. Perhaps I am Nickie Haflinger and I'm riding the shockwave? Who was Nickie Haflinger? He wasn't sure whether he was a fiction or fact – time was out of sync.

'Where am I?'

He knew before he'd asked the question that he'd receive no answer unless it came from the speculative wasteland of his mind. The vastness of this miniscule world overwhelmed him, like a drugged rat locked in a lab-cage, or a skeleton imprisoned in a chest at the bottom of a fathomless ocean.

He floated deeper and further...into space? Inner space? He wasn't sure of anything at all now. He found it hard to recall his own name. Was his own identity being slowly erased?

He tried to command his spinning, drifting body to obey a simple instruction. But the thought to reverse his course and head back the way he had come was nothing more than that – a thought. No action followed. He was helpless; at the mercy of whatever force manoeuvred him through time and space.

He blinked and coughed, but now there was no sound. His cough wasn't dry or hollow. It just didn't exist as sound, except in his head, in his memory that was evaporating quickly.

He span slowly in this miniscule space, like a sperm free-falling after rejection by an egg. He had lost his time sense in this deep, black space, which was changeless. Stars twinkled all about him as distant untouchable specks of glitter.

His mother's watch was frozen at twelve o'clock on his exposed wrist. He glimpsed it now and again, mesmerised by the spider-web pattern of the shattered glass. The concept of time became inconsequential, capitulated. It was as if he was floating out of time in a limitless space that shouldn't be.

Time shifted.

Again.

And again.

Reversed, slipped forward. The hands swirled around the watch-face so fast that they became a colour cartoon blur.

He forgot his mother's face, just couldn't conjure her image in his mind's eye. After an immeasurable amount of non-time, he forgot her name; his father's face and name, and his crew's faces and names. He could not recall his own fame or notoriety, his own contribution to the history of music. His raps were ripped verse by verse, line by line, word by syllable from his recollection until all that was left was a broken alphabet of grunts and hisses and gestures.

He didn't care. Had he ever cared about anyone but himself? He flailed his mind but could not remember. Torture was useless here.

Joey Steffano was being controlled by something unseen, like the antithesis of the wave of light. Yet this unseen force remained gentle – loving almost.

Unconditional. Non-judgemental.

He did not feel hunger, but the raging call of his thirst was deep and unquenchable. His lips felt like they had been blown up by a plastic surgeon, and his palette was parched; tongue sticking to the roof of his mouth. When he occasionally swallowed it was harsh and dry and hurtful.

He longed for a fountain or a cool can of Coke. It didn't come.

He drifted further into space.

Helpless.

Anonymous.

Alone.

2

Yet he didn't feel lonely.

Something was with him, inside him, all around him. He thought of God, of Franklin and his amazing techno-lighted coat, of Mikey J, and the Breakers who'd died on the street in the senseless drive-by shootings. He winced with the pain of absolute recall. He saw elated moments of triumph from his childhood, like when he learned to ride his bike for the first time, or when he wrote his first song. He relived his great disappointments – his mother's drug addiction, the break-up of his family, his friends left behind as he moved from place to place, town to town.

Displaced soul.

Forever relocating.

More memories surfaced, faster and more intense. His head was swirling like a Waltzer.

He was suddenly, horrifically aware that his memory was returning. Like a cog in a machine, each tooth propelled another, squealing with the ecstasy and the pain of total recollection. Cog and wheel and tooth and motion – circular, locked, powerful. Slow and deliberate. His memory came flooding back and with it a zoo of emotions.

He cried out into the abyss. His tiny voice was obliterated by the silence and darkness for a moment and then it erupted like a deep sea earthquake.

He screamed at the shockwave of his own voice. It was harsh and loud and round.

He had felt secure and warm in the drifting, voiceless void of space. He wanted to return. There was no pressure there, no strain, no stress and no expectations.

It was a waking sleep.

But then a new thought entered his mind: he was still being controlled by an unseen hand. That hand may have been God or David Blaine's hypno-trip, or it may have been genetic instinct; hell it could have been the motion of a leaf falling from an autumnal tree for all he knew.

Anything.

Everything.

Whatever.

It really didn't matter. What mattered was his memory. That had returned wholesale. Complete. And even though he recalled all those terrible things he'd said and thought and done, he also saw the better things, the selfless things, the generosity of his actions and words. His music was his key. He'd brought happiness and inspiration to unknown millions. People he'd never seen, never met, or would never encounter. They had listened to his music, to his rhyming words, his rap, to his opinions, his loves and hates, hopes and fears, and it had touched them in ways that he could only speculate.

Good things he had done.

Bad things he had done.

The light didn't judge. The light cleaned and repaired

and heightened. The light was a good friend in the deep dark of timelessness and space. But it was also the enemy of hateful thoughts and actions.

Hurtful words and conversations he'd had with so many people, fans, his mum and step-dad, his manager, Jack O'Toole, everyone he'd ever encountered for more than an hour, these painful words stuck to him like nicotine patches. He sweated and shouted abuse, cursed and tried to rip the words from his flesh but they stuck. They stung him repeatedly like a swarm of wasps. These words were living things. He felt the pain they had inflicted upon others and he knew the harm he had done was a bad thing.

But the light clarified his hurt.

It was bigger than anything he'd ever experienced before. It didn't judge, or forgive, or sanctify. It cleansed. It was a benediction. A blessing so far removed from religious connotations, so far away from the temple or church or mosque, so far removed from man-made religion or holy books that its stark simplicity overwhelmed him.

He felt like a small child hiding beneath a table, hoping not to be seen by the adults walking by. He felt as if he'd been singled out by his father and made to stand before a crowd and speak in a language foreign to him.

He was overwhelmed totally.

3

Then it was over. He was no longer floating aimlessly in deep space, galaxies his companions. He was back.

4

Joey Steffano opened his eyes as the root snapped, and the entity lost its grip and plunged into the wormhole. Time had reversed, or perhaps he'd simply returned to a moment before his deep space journey had begun because that was the location that made most sense to him, grounded him in what was partially familiar.

Whatever.

The earth filled the void.

Gone.

Just an indent where the hole had been.

Still screaming, pleading for mercy as it tumbled into the well of light. Joey squinted at the grotesque features and thought for a moment that he recognised himself in the creature's wild, panicked eyes.

Joey stepped back, dazed, legs slack beneath him. His Nike trainers were encrusted with mud. He staggered sideways and whirled around. He glimpsed Franklin, closing his coat. Light shrank as if a dimmer switch had been twisted. Then the light was gone, hidden, and Franklin buttoned his leather coat.

They followed Franklin. Harry, Ellen and the children who'd been rescued from the smoke trudged across the wasteland to the train in stunned silence. The zigzagging bolts of electricity (that's what Joey presumed they were, but he had no way of knowing) crackled and spat and vanished.

The train doors whooshed open.

He was the last one to step into the train, turning to glimpse the twilight and smoke behind him. Franklin grabbed his elbow and helped him onboard, a steadying hand for his quivering legs.

'You look pale, son,' he said. 'Perhaps you should take it easy for awhile. Come on. Let's sit down.'

Joey did as Franklin said. He felt no resistance to this man anymore.

'I feel weird, different,' Joey said.

'Sure, son. You just take it easy now.'

'I'm really thirsty. Is there any water onboard this train?'

'Best not to drink until you get to Journey's End, son. There's something wrong with the water supply onboard.'

Joey knew the old guy was hiding something, but it didn't seem to matter anymore. He felt so very different, remade, childlike.

'What's wrong?'

'Not sure. We had to turn off the taps.'

Joey recalled how he'd tried but failed to get a drink from the washbasin. 'So tired and thirsty,' he said. 'I need to sleep.'

'Sure. No problem, son. Relax. Chill.'

Chillax. Joey heard Mikey J in his head.

'How far are we from Journey's End?' Joey heard himself saying, his voice sounding thick, distant, vague.

'Not far, son. Just a couple of Sector stops to make first. You sleep. I'll wake you when we arrive.'

'Can I help?' Joey heard himself saying, then...

The hip-hop star slept.

Franklin leaned across and held his glowing fingertips over the infected flesh around the silver dollar. He tugged and the coin released like a dead tooth in a dentist's hand.

There was a hole in Joey's head, deep and dark. But soon light would come to fill it and it would heal, probably with no scar at all.

Gently, Franklin J Merryhill slipped the silver dollar into one of Joey's many pockets.

'A souvenir, son,' he said. 'Sleep well. Dream happy dreams. Embrace the love of the light.'

Had Joey been able to recall his transition from his present state of consciousness to another, he would have perceived a fraught and, at times, confusing train journey. As it was, he saw a vast tunnel of light, which engulfed him, penetrated, illuminated and redefined, remade, and healed him from the inside out.

The light was everywhere, shimmering.

And standing at the far, far tapered point of Journey's End, he saw a figure dressed in a flat cap, flannel work jacket, baggy work trousers and gardening boots covered in mud. That figure's beaming smile and outstretched arms extended toward him.

'Good to see you, son,' said the figure.

Wiping tears of joy and relief from his eyes with the back of his hand, Joey said one word: 'Grand-dad.'

It was a small word, but it meant everything to Joey Steffano.